THE INTERNATIONAL
KILLER THRILLER

THE INTERNATIONAL KILLER THRILLER

Daniel Silva's Reinvention
of Spy and Noir Fiction

Annabel Patterson

Library of Congress Control Number:		2017902410
ISBN:	Hardcover	978-1-5245-8420-7
	Softcover	978-1-5245-8419-1
	eBook	978-1-5245-8418-4

Print information available on the last page.

Rev. date: 03/14/2017

Images curated by Caitlin Woolsey

To order additional copies of this book, contact:
Xlibris
1-888-795-4274
www.Xlibris.com
Orders@Xlibris.com
754013

CONTENTS

Ireland

Syria

The International
Killer Thriller

On Tuesday, March 22, 2016, simultaneous terrorist attacks in Belgium, one of the world's littlest and most harmless countries, made human havoc of the Brussels airport and a metro station. There were at least six suicide bombers, and "credit" for the well-planned attack was claimed by the new Islamic "state," Isis. On November 13, 2015, Isis-linked extremists attacked the Bataclan concert hall and other sites across Paris. This violence was alarmingly well synchronized, the choice of targets was shrewd, and the death toll was 130. On July 2005, 52 commuters were killed in London by 4 suicide bombers in 3 subway trains and a bus. Back then, it was Al-Qaeda running the show. And of course, it was fanatical Al-Qaeda pilots who, on September 11, 2001, turned their planes and themselves into the most lethal of bombs to take down the Twin Towers in New York, thus showing that America's physical distance was no protection from terrorism spawned in the Middle East. Osama bin Laden himself exulted over the success of this mission.

In 2011, Daniel Silva, an increasingly lauded novelist, released his *Portrait of a Spy*, his eleventh of the so-called espionage novels. It opens with three terrorist attacks, by single suicide bombers, in Paris, Copenhagen, and London's Covent Garden. These are followed by a car bombing in a busy street in Spain, which after the dreadful nonfictional attack in March 2004 on a Madrid railway station had, according to Silva, been trying to protect itself by withdrawing its troops from Iraq and redirecting Muslim rage toward America. This did not protect it against the fictional but lethal follow-up that Silva scheduled for 2011.

Although thousands of people have been reading Silva, they may not have been reading him proactively. Silva's hero, Gabriel Allon, is a Jew and a world-famous assassin employed by Israeli security. Silva is one of the very few novelists who skirt the dangerous shores of contemporaneity, of writing up to the moment. Published in 2011, *Portrait of a Spy* establishes *its* moment as just after the fall of Mubarak in Egypt, which occurred in November of that year. The novel's thesis is that there is now a successor to Al-Qaeda, a "new network that had yet to produce a blip on the radar screen of Western intelligence." In Silva's hypothesis, which was published *before* the formation of Isis in April 2013, the persons behind the attacks were a couple of masterminds, one with a silver tongue, the other a ruthless killer, who banded together to set up terrorist cells all over the world, including three in the United States. These cells are eliminated by a clever trick to "follow the money." Mindful of how carefully one must step not to become a spoiler, I will say merely that the money was donated by a Saudi heiress. This part of the story is all fictional, if prophetic and advisory. Prophetic in that its description of the new jihadist network applies just as well or better to Isis than to Al-Qaeda, "an organized force that seeks to weaken or even destroy the West through acts of indiscriminate violence . . . part of a broader radical movement to impose sharia law and restore the Islamic Caliphate" (p. 80). These are the words of Silva's fictional Adrian Carter, the director of the CIA's clandestine service. They are also advisory in that Carter is dubious about the U.S. president's desire (obviously Obama's) to redirect America's efforts from the war on terrorism to more fruitful and winnable projects (p. 81). And in 2011, in both real and fictional time, Osama bin Laden was killed, an event the novel alludes to (p. 274).

This is exactly where we stand today, in real time. Osama bin Laden is really dead. But under Abu Musab al-Zarqawi, a new terrorist organization has been set up with its roots in the U.S. invasion of Iraq. The group, made up of Sunnis, began by targeting Shiites. However, when Paul Bremer, the American sent to Iraq by Bush to settle the now headless country, disbanded its entire governing structure, including that of the army, hundreds of displaced and disgusted men were available for recruitment. And recruited they were. Under a new leader, Abu Bakr al-Baghdadi, Isis expanded its objectives from sectarian attacks and, in 2013, announced its goal to create an international caliphate. It now had the army and the weapons to make that more than just talk. Even so conservative a conservative as Newt Gingrich called Bremer "the largest single disaster in American foreign policy in modern times."

In 2014, two years ago, I published a book titled *The International Novel*, a survey of novels written by people, some famous, some almost unheard of in the West, who wanted to stake their claim, the claim of *their* nation, not only to the territory of important fiction but also to the increasingly tendentious discussion of *nationalism*. What did nationalism offer in a postcolonial, postimperial world; and what developments did it inhibit? Deliberately short and only slightly theoretical, the book set its face against what then seemed a dangerous mistake, to forsake a nuanced and up-to-date discussion of nationalism for the broad intellectual smear and all-purpose excuse of globalism as something largely financial in nature and happening beyond our control. I now revoke that position. Globalism is with us for better or worse and mostly the latter. And it is beyond our control. But if I revoke that position, I retain my trust in the novel—the international novel—to put it to us plainly. In *Portrait of a Spy*, the most obvious cause of an unwanted globalism was "the belief that Europe could absorb an endless tide of Muslim immigrants from its former colonies while preserving its culture and basic way of life" (p. 12). Apparently, nobody noticed this warning. In September 2015, three years after *Portrait of a Spy* was published, Angela Merkel, the German chancellor, responded to the civil war in Syria by opening her country's door and, hence, the doors of other countries in the European Union. Little thought was given as to how difficult it would be to sort genuine refugees (those who had been living in extreme danger) from torrents of economic migrants braving the deserts and the seas for "a better life." The "endless tide" still rises.

I do not seriously claim that Merkel should have heeded the warning of a novelist. Common sense would have served. I do claim that the novels of Daniel Silva are, first, very broadly international in their concerns; and second, that they contain, within the alluring structure of brilliantly plotted thrillers, valid information about the current state of the world, which our politicians must attempt to negotiate: Syria, Saudi Arabia, the Emirates, Iraq, Iran, Turkey, Lebanon, Italy, the United Kingdom, Russia, and, of course, Israel and Palestine. Switzerland keeps reappearing in a most unflattering light. The penultimate novel, *The English Spy*, deals with the deadly afterlife of Irish terrorism and its long reach.

It is customary to see Silva as a worthy successor to John Le Carré. But despite certain titles, *The English Spy* and *Portrait of a Spy*, Silva's novels are not really about espionage. His first book, the one that was an instant success and generated the sequence, was titled *The Kill Artist*. The second was *The English Assassin*. Gabriel makes no bones about the fact that he is an assassin in the service and the pay of Israel. Israel thinks its cause is just. When is an assassin a necessary means to a righteous end, and when is he a terrorist? Using the term "terrorist" is a way to delegitimize our new enemies in the Middle East. Of course, an assassin only kills one or two people at a time, whereas terrorists engage in mass murder. Readers should be able to follow this thought further. This problem will not go away, and each new novel in the Gabriel Allon series raises some version of it. These novels should be reclassified as "Killer Thrillers," and readers should be aware of the tension, what is thrilling and what is chilling.

This book of mine reopens the premise that sometimes works of fiction—novels—can do important work in the world, especially if they are profound and especially if they are troubled about their own assumptions. If world leaders read Silva or read him differently, they might have been better prepared to deal with the war in Syria and its fallout across Europe. As for the ordinary reader, you can become much better informed globally while thoroughly enjoying yourself. No pain, great gain.

To date, Silva has written twenty thrillers, seventeen of which feature Gabriel Allon, Jewish assassin. Allon means oak tree in Hebrew, which may be vaguely reassuring, suggesting deep roots. *The Kill Artist* (1998) faced these questions directly in its title and conducted a mild debate on the differences, if any, between justice and revenge, between assassin and terrorist, and between "enhanced interrogation" and torture. The justice/revenge choice stems from the fact that Allon's first assignment was to hunt down and shoot the Palestinian terrorists who killed the Jewish athletes at the Munich Olympic Games. He killed them separately; if they had all been on one bus, would that have been terrorism too?

The other theme of the Allon novels, which has a mitigating effect on the violence, is also advertised in the first novel's title, *The Kill Artist*, because when Gabriel is not hunting down the bad guys, he is restoring old masters. As a restorer, he is also world famous; he is often employed by the Vatican or by the most adorable of characters, Julian Isherwood, who owns a gallery in London. But the *idea* of restoration underpins all the novels as a metaphor for setting things straight. The descriptions of fictional paintings on which Gabriel agrees to work substitute for real old masters very like them, and one can take pleasure recognizing the true in the somewhat askew. Gabriel can also forge paintings—of course, in a good cause. Needless to say, the metaphor of restoration underpins all the novels. As an artist, Gabriel commands our respect; and we sympathize with him because his restoration assignments, which he much prefers, keep getting interrupted or actually derailed by his other responsibilities. But Silva insists on revisiting the gray area between acceptable and unacceptable violence; and unfortunately, almost all the novels involve Gabriel's putting a woman at great risk and only rescuing her after she has suffered severe damage.

There is a huge advantage in writing a series of novels with the same protagonist and the same or almost the same cast of surrounding characters, such as Julian Isherwood, the tragicomic gallery owner, or Graham Seymour, the British espiocrat. We come to care about them or hate them. But this advantage is nearly offset by one of the few flaws of the Allon novels, which is that each time a member of the supporting cast reappears, he or she has to be reintroduced in case the reader has not started at the beginning of the series. But if she has, these reintroductions, often in the same words as their first incarnations, are seriously obsolete. She turns the page with a sigh. The other grave problem of having a series of novels develop over seventeen fictional years, which themselves run nearly parallel to real years, is that one's hero and those around him must age. In *The Confessor*, the third novel, Gabriel is just fifty-one in the fictional year 2003. Therefore, in the fictional year 2015, the date of *The English Spy*, he should be twelve years older, that is, sixty-three, time to settle down to the desk job as chief of security in Israel, which he has finally agreed to take on, and rather late to be on the verge of having twins, imminent at the end of *The English Spy*. Because of the carefully arranged sense of closure in *The English Spy*—the new job, the new twins, and the return of Christopher Keller, Allon's partner in assassination or its prevention to a legal life, to Graham Seymour's M16, to London, and to his elderly parents, who have long believed him dead—readers may be prepared to countenance the fact of Allon's superannuation. What then will they say to the Author's promise on page 519 of "the next installment in the series"?

TRUTH AND FICTION

Daniel Silva performs in these fifteen novels a dangerous dance between the alternatives we loosely know as Truth and Fiction, a dance that intensifies the reader's pleasure. He claims, of course, that any resemblance to persons, living or dead, "is entirely coincidental." This is the old trick that writers have used for centuries to avoid repercussions, the trick that in *Censorship and Interpretation* I called the disclaimer. But here, the disclaimer is itself a fiction. The American presidents—Clinton, Bush, and Obama—are not only identifiable, but they are also actually named in the Author's Notes. More importantly, the horrific picture of Vladimir Putin that gradually emerges over three novels becomes blatant in the late *The English Spy*, wherein some of Silva's strongest warnings about the future are embedded. Yasir Arafat appears in his own person in *The Kill Artist*, and a surprisingly sympathetic person, at a moment before he scuttled Clinton's peace accord by refusing to sign it. Then there is Gabriel's mentor and commander, Ari Shamron, who seems unavoidably related to the controversial Israeli general, defense minister, and prime minister, Ariel Sharon. Shamron's steely vigilance in defense of his country is a device to shelter Gabriel from our revulsion. It was Sharon as defense minister who enabled the terrible massacres of Palestinians in 1983 in the Sabra and Shatila refugee camps, for which he was forced to resign. As we work our way or play our way through the novels, we will encounter many more characters or events that require us to apply the "truth" test by the use of elementary research, a process that is itself highly educative. Thus, the opening terrorist attack on the Israeli embassy in Rome in *Prince of Fire* turns out to be only a fiction; but discovering this leads to a much sadder truth, of how many attacks on embassies, especially though not exclusively of the United States, there actually were since 1979. To invent one for an Israeli embassy therefore might seem to be special pleading. It makes a great start for a novel, but it is sort of cheating. I will return to this dilemma in the final chapter.

But one of the most interesting strategies that Silva uses to confuse the issue of historical truthfulness is his *invention* of a pope, not just any pope but a liberal reformer who seeks to redeem his church from centuries of anti-Semitism. Set in fictional 2003, *The Confessor* begins a long friendship between the (obviously) Catholic pope and Gabriel, the Israeli Jew. Then ten years before the 2013 election of Pope Francis, the most liberal pope the church has chosen in a century, Silva imagines an old man of great conscience, whose plan to counter anti-Semitism at least in his own domain and to open the Vatican and its secrets to the world nearly gets him killed. This too was prophecy, not of the danger to the pope but of the power of an office repaired, reconstructed. Gabriel's invented pope was Italian, Pietro Lucchese, with a fairy-tale biography carefully withheld till the end of the story. He chose the name of Paul VII, and he was a compromise candidate. The hard-liners had wanted another kind of Italian altogether, "a consummate creature of the Roman Curia," the current Secretary of the Vatican state. The moderates believed the time had come for a Third-World Pope. How prescient!

As we work our way through the novels, following not only the brilliant plots but also the conversations about ethics in a world falling apart, we may come to believe that Silva is determined to make us rethink our own attitudes to Zionism. This process has been very hard for me. It has certainly sensitized me to the moments of doubt, of guilt, and of protesting too much by the Israeli characters and the laments or self-justifications of the Palestinians, so many of which I have selected for quotation and/ or commentary. Here, the boundary between fact and fiction is more than a literary trick. It requires the reader to create for him or herself a confessional relationship to the text, a *working* relationship, one that will allow for changes of mind as we move through the series, hoping for fiction yet demanding truth.

THE KILL ARTIST:
PERSONAL VENGEANCE

Obviously, he prefers his women damaged.

—The Confessor

This first novel in the Gabriel Allon series featured a new protagonist for Silva, whose three previous ones had featured British-type spies without Allon's ethnic and ethical complexity, rather obviously in the shadow of John Le Carré. The huge success of the first Allon book seems to have taken Silva a little by surprise since it took four years for its successor, *The English Assassin*, to appear. Thereafter, the Allon books came out annually, to greater and greater applause. One reviewer noted that the thrillers took "a hard look at serious issues" (*The Washington Post*) as well as doing what thrillers are supposed to do: grip the reader in an iron grasp from start to finish. *The Kill Artist* opens literally with a bang, juxtaposing Gabriel's honorable career as a restorer of old masterpieces with the event that would continue to haunt him for the rest of his life: the blowing up of the car containing his wife, Leah, and his little boy, two-year-old Dani (Daniel). This horrific personal event, as we will learn later, is doubly terrible for Gabriel because it was his affair with a bat *leveyah* (the Hebrew word for female accomplice) that has brought his wife to Vienna and exposed her to vengeance from the opposite side: the bomber Tariq, significantly not a suicide bomber, was retaliating for Gabriel's killing of his brother, who had been a member of Black September, the group who captured and then killed the Israeli athletes at the Munich Olympics in 1972. The scene of Leah and Dani's death is dated January 1991, almost two decades later. But the burned and psychologically damaged Leah and the dead Dani will haunt Gabriel in novel after novel in a way that makes my opening quotation, appearing two novels *later* and dropped casually by a mildly jealous woman, seem fearsomely significant. It will turn out to be prescient as well since Gabriel has a habit of recruiting women for the most dangerous exploits.

Silva chooses 1998 as the main fictional time of the novel, conveniently also the date of its publication. In this strange "present," Tariq then reappears as the main antagonist, who has just done something terrible to get back on Israel's blacklist. He has successfully carried out the assassination of the Israeli ambassador to France. Consequently, Shamron has summoned Gabriel back from England, where he had eagerly begun the restoration of a Vecellio altarpiece. Tone is everything at this point, and the tone of Gabriel's recall is established by the presence of a child in the Cornwall village, where Gabriel has secluded himself for his work. The child is called Timothy Peel, and he is about the same age as Gabriel's son would have been by now, that is, seven years after Dani's death. Timothy adopts Gabriel as a mysterious father figure (his own father had divorced his mother), and the two strike up a simple rural friendship more important to the child than the artist, alas. From this honest and innocent moment, Gabriel is recalled by Shamron; and he unwillingly enters the very urban world of London streets and apartments, where spying on a man (with no particular evidence of his wrongdoing) is accomplished by the new technology, whereby anyone can spy on anyone even in his own home.

Now Tariq is clearly a dangerous man, but he happens to be dying from a brain tumor. He is not a mass murderer. He might have been left to die alone. He does have a large destructive motive, however, that is, to derail the peace process currently being orchestrated by the American president, who in real time must be Bill Clinton. And here, the ethical choices are articulated. Gabriel asks reasonably what the killing of the ambassador has to do with him. Shamron, in reply, quotes Ezekiel: "And the enemy shall know I am Lord when I can lay down my vengeance upon them." And he continues, "I believe that if someone kills one of my people, I should kill him in return. Do you believe that, Gabriel?" Gabriel replies, rather evasively, "I used to believe it." "My point," continues Shamron, "is that revenge is good. Revenge is healthy. Revenge is purifying." Clearly, he had never read *Hamlet* or any of the revenge tragedies of the seventeenth century, nor had he considered by what right he could speak for the God of Ezekiel. Gabriel's response is clearly the "right" one, even more so within the Israeli-Palestinian conflict than perhaps ever or anywhere before: "Revenge only leads to more killing and more revenge. For every terrorist we kill, there's another boy waiting to step forward and pick up the sword or the gun. They're like sharks' teeth; break one and another will rise in its place." This is a message that George W. Bush signally failed to understand.

Alas, Gabriel does not adhere to his own common sense; had he done so, there would have been no novel. Back in London, he engages in an unwise reprise of the past and recruits as his assistant the very woman, Sarah Halevy, who indirectly had caused the destruction of his family. Now a famous London model, renamed Jacqueline Delacroix to conceal her Jewish roots, his bat *leveyah* from the episode in Tunis is recalled to duty. She is willing to do that, first, because she is still in love with Gabriel and hopes to win him back and second, because her career as a model is falling victim to her own aging process; and in her early thirties, she is already on the downward slope. So she puts herself in serious danger. That she survives physically is pretty much implicit in the genre, but at the end of the story, she is reduced to living in complete isolation in a beach resort in Israel, the first or the second of Gabriel's damaged women.

Trying as best I can to avoid giving away the plot, which is what most readers are concerned about, I shall focus only on Silva's intellectual aims, if one can call something so confusing an aim. Of course, vengeance against Tariq must be filtered in as well as Sharon's concerns. Since Jacqueline's job is to ensnare in a honey trap a man who represents Palestine in the novel's iconography (but we can't actually be certain about that), sexual tension and deceit stand in for the endless conflict between the two nations. She is to get close to a young Palestinian, whom Gabriel believes to be working for Tariq; but in the course of her seduction, she herself will be subjected to a political reeducation mostly conducted in bed. This will require some long quotations:

> *I'm afraid you have fallen for the great Zionist myth, Dominique [Yusef speaking]. The myth that the Palestinians would voluntarily trade where they had lived for centuries for*

exile and refugee camps . . . Do you want to know why my family ended up in a camp in Beirut (Lebanon)? . . . We call it al-Nakba. The catastrophe . . . When the United Nations presented the plan to partition Palestine into two states, the Jews realized they had a serious problem. The Zionists had come to Palestine to build a Jewish state, but nearly half of the people in the new partition state were to be Arabs. The Jews accepted the partition plan, knowing full well that it would be unacceptable to the Arabs . . . The Jews owned seven percent of Palestine, but they were being handed fifty percent of the country, including the most fertile land along the coastal plain and the Upper Galilee . . . The Jews devised a plan to remove the Arabs from the land designated for the Jewish state. They even had a name for it: Plan Dalet.

Not being in bed with either party, we should inform ourselves of the "truth." Not as simple as one might hope. Plan Dalet (D) had a perfectly factual, historical existence in that on April 9, 1948, a massacre occurred in Deir Yassin, an Arab village of approximately six hundred people, near Jerusalem and part of the new administrative unit that was supposed in future to govern the holy city. The motives for the attack, the identity of those ultimately responsible, and of course, even the number of those killed immediately became something to fight over, a propaganda campaign that established the fight as also between fact and fiction. Israel's sixth prime minister, Menachem Begin, was then leader of Irgun, one of the two extremist military groups that broke away from the Haganah, the main Jewish militia. The other was the Lehi, and both were aligned with right-wing Zionist groups. Both Irgun and Lehi were involved in the massacre, and Haganah was complicit in the planning. The villagers were not without arms, and there was fierce resistance; but that women and children were killed, some women raped, and that looting was taken for granted seem inarguable. Begin later lauded the event and confirmed that its intended effect, causing Palestinian villages elsewhere to empty out, had indeed occurred: "Not what happened at Deir Yassan, but what was *invented about* Deir Yassan," continued Yusef, "helped to carve the way to our decisive victories on the battlefield . . . The legend was worth half a dozen battalions to the forces of Israel." In other words, the massacre was planned in terrorem.

But the instruction of Dominique in Israeli/Palestinian conflict does not end with the initial scandal of Deir Yassan. To punch the message home, Yusef claims that his own family came from the village of Lydda, which no longer exists: "It is now Lod, where the Zionists put their fucking airport." Here too, a major expulsion of Palestinians, preceded by a massacre, has been a historian's nightmare not only in counting the dead and explaining the mass departure of the inhabitants of Lydda and also Ramle in 1948 but also in determining who, if anyone, signed off on the action. By some extraordinary coincidence, which is probably anything but, the modern account divides responsibility among Prime Minister David Ben-Gurion, who had an obsession with the Arab towns; Yitzhak Rabin, who acknowledged the "driving out" in his memoirs (subsequently pruned of this episode by an Israeli censorship board); and Yigal Allon, commanding officer of Operation Dani, as it was called. Allon himself declared that there had been no expulsions—the Arabs left voluntarily, but the talk was that Allon had a scorched earth policy where the Palestinians were concerned. How are we to relate these names, Allon and Dani, to the story we are currently engaged with?

What was Dominique's response? "I had no idea." I too had no idea until reading the Silva text made me search for the "truth," which in these two instances is nowhere certainly to be found. All we have are intensely partisan accounts, which scarcely deserve the title of records. And then as if this were not more than enough, Yusef tells Dominique he had previously lied about how he got the terrible scar on his back. He had been wounded at the 1982 massacre of Palestinian refugees in the Lebanese camps of Sabra and Shatila, where the Phalangists, the "Christian" militia, dragged him behind a car, using him for shooting practice. In the meantime, they had brutally murdered his mother and his little sister. The toll of the murdered was up to two thousand refugees—men, women, children, and infants. The ultimate responsibility for this had been laid at the door of Ariel Sharon, who had sent the Phalangists into the camps without supervision and with only the loosest of orders. When Dominique reports back to Gabriel about this news, the two have an angry debate, which continues that between Gabriel and Shamron earlier. But now Gabriel is channeling Shamron, and Dominique is taking Gabriel's earlier position.

Jaqueline protests, "Why didn't you tell me his family had been butchered like that?" And Gabriel replies, "He's suffered. So what? We've all suffered. It doesn't give him the right to murder innocent people because history didn't go his way . . . Now is not the time for a debate on moral equivalence and the ethics of counterterrorism." When the quarrel refocuses on Tariq, Jaqueline asks the central question about revenge: "When does it end, Gabriel? When there's no more blood to shed?" But this for her is just a rhetorical question, assuaging her conscience. She could, of course, escape the operation at this point; but she won't because she is fixated on Gabriel himself.

Moral equivalence and the ethics of counterterrorism? When *will* there be a debate—an international debate—on this question? When is a man about to commit murder a warrior prince (which is how Shamron likes to think of Gabriel), and when is he simply another terrorist? How do we define terrorism? That which produces terror? In whom? This first Gabriel Allon novel raises these questions in a more painful form, by way of filling out the Palestinian viewpoint and the historical (true) events that created it, than any of the novels that succeed it, let alone moral equivalence. This book stages in what was in 1998 a painfully timely form, extreme ambivalence. One can hardly enjoy the novelistic device of a "successful" completion of the story, not least because Gabriel is nearly killed during the finale, something that happens a great many time in the series. Are his multiple injuries and recoveries a new spin on fiction's old assumption that a mythic hero (prince or archangel) must die in the performance of his victory or at least suffer terribly? Keep reading, please, and at least asking, if not answering, these questions.

ISRAEL AND PALESTINE:
THE HOLOCAUST SERIES

THE ENGLISH ASSASSIN

The English Assassin is the first of three novels in which Daniel Silva showed the world that he had much more to offer beyond *The Kill Artist*. Indeed, in the "Author's Notes" to *A Death in Venice*, we learn that it is the first of a series of three Holocaust novels. They deal not in the event itself but with the cultural and moral aftermath of the Holocaust, a subject of intense interest to Israel and to half of the rest of the world. In these three novels, Silva expanded his geographical reach to include most of Europe, including especially Switzerland; Italy, especially Venice and the Vatican; Austria; Spain (particularly Lisbon); and Germany. These were some of the areas in which the espionage novels of Alan Furst were sited, although each of those had a different protagonist and was situated within or just after World War II. Silva's are contemporary with us and face the remains or the return of anti-Semitism in Europe. Meanwhile, their geographical diversity adds sophistication—cosmopolitanism—especially since Silva has a marvelous ability to give his readers a visual sense of the cities in question.

And now Silva developed the redeeming theme of Gabriel Allon's other pursuit, restoring old paintings, which had been only metaphorically active in *The Kill Artist*. *The English Assassin* deals with the sad story of a Swiss banker who had accumulated a treasure trove of valuable modern paintings via his relationship with Heimlich Himmler and Adolf Hitler, a stolen and then re-stolen collection. Some of these are eventually returned to the heirs of their Jewish owners. Thus, paintings open the way for a reinspection of the leading Nazis's rapacious appetite for art, a lust that they were able to satisfy by looting and phony purchasing. Gabriel would have called this "opening a window" in a dirty canvas to see what underlies it. This book does not indulge us with a verbal viewing of any particular paintings or ekphrasis. The next two in the series, though, feature famous paintings that are still in place—both by Bellini, both altarpieces, and both in Venice churches: *The Virgin and Child with Saints* in San Zaccaria and *Saints Christopher, Jerome, and Louis of Toulouse* in San Giovanni Crisostomo. Though not all of Gabriel's saved or restored paintings in later novels are "real" in the same sense, these can be seen not only in their original locations but also online, making it possible to analyze their thematic relationship to their frame novels.

The English Assassin features no single actual painting but rather the idea of paintings as objects of value in World War II, objects that represent the violation of social norms destroyed by the Nazis, norms signified by ownership. This is a problem to which Silva will return in later novels and, of course, one which continues to plague museums and individuals who have acquired art of dubious or no provenance. In this novel, stolen art stands for and is a figure for the complete deracination or eradication of Jewish property at the moment houses were ransacked through to that end when gold teeth were gouged out of Jewish corpses. A subordinate theme is the recently developed ethic that private collections of paintings are a violation of the central principles of what make art valuable: openness, or sharing, or education. And at the far end of *The English Assassin* is a Gothic representation of this ethical issue, unlikely to be solved in our time, not least because some of the new hoarders are in the Middle East.

In broadening, deepening, and geographically widening his canvas, Silva was clearly appealing to audiences not particularly concerned with the Israeli/Palestinian conflict. But he also apparently tried to redeem the guilt-ridden protagonist of *The Kill Artist*. This story features Gabriel *not* as an assassin but a rescuer and protector. In this case, he does not deploy a woman in a destructive operation but saves her from another assassin, a mysterious figure named Christopher Keller, who kills for hire. This man is called the English Assassin because he, like some art, has no provenance. Keller/Killer. We will meet him again in other novels, where he changes his symbolic value, proving to be an extremely amusing person who is obviously worth restoration. In this novel already, he is revealed as having a conscience. The woman in question is Anna Rolfe, a famous violinist already damaged by the time Gabriel encounters her, both because she has witnessed her mother's suicide and because, isolating herself on a hilltop in Portugal, she has been caught in a storm and a landslide that seriously wounded her essential left hand. Gabriel has nothing to do with restoration of her hand and her musician's confidence, but he takes her under his protection and ensures or tries to ensure that nobody will harm her when she reenters the world of performance. Note that the demanding piece by Tartini, "The Devil's Trill," which she successfully plays on that occasion, is a real and famous musical challenge.

Creating an English assassin as an antagonist to Gabriel relieves him of that title, and the tone of this novel is far less guilty; or rather, the guilt is reassigned. Those who die are not killed by Gabriel. Here, we also make the acquaintance of Gabriel's team (now he has backup), some of whose names and features will reappear thereafter. And perhaps more importantly still, Gabriel is not sent on this mission by Shamron but steps into it by mistake, literally stepping into the blood of Anna's father, shed by someone who does not want the secret hoard of paintings in his possession opened up like the can of worms it is. The mission is innocently initiated by my favorite character, Julian Isherwood, gallery owner, whose role it is to track down forgotten or unvalued paintings and get them back on view. Anna's assassination at her most important concert had been planned by a Swiss villain, who has his own huge, hidden collection, never to be seen by any eyes at all, including his own, planned but thwarted because the English Assassin turns out to have a conscience. Switzerland's role in holing up Nazi acquisitions is the main theme here, and it resonates still today in what will go down in history under the title of the Panama Papers. Swiss banks have been forced to open up though not before this novel was published; but the opportunity for the rich to secrete their riches abroad is, if anything, a greater problem for international relations. In this too, Silva's work is both prophetic and timely.

Also introduced in this novel is the Corsica element, which is fun not only because of the amiable Corsican don who runs a profitable business of "Murder for Hire" (supposed to be a modern improvement on the old system of vendetta, which was never-ending) but also because of the goat. I will let you encounter the goat—and encounter is the right word—for yourselves. In this novel, Gabriel is on the Don's list for elimination, along with Anna. The other memorable character from this region, who will have several appearances in the Allon series, is an old woman with magic powers, the *signadora*. She can see both past and future and has the ability to cleanse those in whom she is interested, who include both Keller and Gabriel, from the evil eye. That is to say, from the evil aspect of what they do, either for a living or because events demand it. An unorthodox redemption.

If that is too magical for you, there is "Realism" here too in what will become Silva's signature blend of fact and fiction. Obviously, the role of the Swiss bankers in facilitating the looting of Jewish possessions is a fact and one acknowledged by a seven-year independent commission that reported in August 2001. This might have been the event that generated the novel, published in 2002. But other Swiss history plays an explicit role here too. On page 281, the narrator inserts the story of the founding of the Swiss republic in 1291 in the Rütli meadow on the shores of Lake Lucerne:

> *In 1291, the leaders of the three so-called Forest Cantons . . . are said to have gathered in the Rütli Meadows and formed a defensive alliance against anyone who "may plot evil against their persons or goods." The event is sacred to the Swiss. A mural of the Rütli Meadow adorns the wall of the Swiss National Council Chamber, and each August the meeting on the meadow is remembered with a national day of celebration.*

At this point, fact gives way to fiction. "Seven hundred years later, a similar defensive alliance was formed by a group of the country's richest and most powerful bankers and industrialists. They called themselves the Council of Rütli and their leader was Otto Gessler" (p. 282). No longer at all pastoral, this new alliance, Silva claims, was formed for self-defense against the charges now being investigated about Switzerland's role in assisting the Nazis while enriching itself. Its goal was maintaining absolute secrecy by any means. Naturally, there is no trace of such an organization in the records. It might have existed; it might not. But as part of the agile footwork that Silva maintains between history and fiction, he draws for his villain's name on another Swiss heroic legend, the story of William Tell, who in the twelfth century defeated the hateful Austrian tyrant Gessler by safely shooting an apple off his son's head and later shooting Gessler himself. This allusion by way of naming is both light-footed and quite visible so that the reader can easily decipher the move.

THE CONFESSOR

The next year appeared *The Confessor*. It continues the Holocaust theme of its predecessor by accomplishing, as mentioned in my first chapter, Silva's most daring and prophetic fiction: the creation of the best pope ever, one who is determined to attack residual anti-Semitism at its heart, which was, of course, age-old church doctrine. We quickly learn that belief and doctrine and practice are the theme of this novel but not in the way we might expect. In the very first scene, a hired assassin, a man called either Eric Lange or "The Leopard," offers his victim, Benjamin Stern, whom he has already mortally wounded, a Catholic absolution, in Latin "Ego te absolvo a peccatis tuis . . ." Whereupon Stern, about to die, complains about the impropriety of such a religious statement at a moment like this and the wrong religion at that. "But I'm a Jew," he murmured. "It doesn't matter," the assassin said. The sharp conflict between murder and religious absolution applied by the murderer to his victim begins a whole series of questions for the reader about the role of religion in world history. "It doesn't matter?"

From that astonishing beginning, we go to meet Paul VII or Pietro Lucchese, only recently elevated to the position by a close vote in the Curia and already generating secret and dangerous opposition because of his determination to open the Vatican archives for inspection. As *The English Assassin* had turned on the role of the Swiss in World War II, so *The Confessor* turned on the role of the Catholic Church during that same war, which was despicable. The mystery explored in this novel is just how despicable it was, why Benjamin Stern was murdered, and that sets going an even more astonishing sequence of events that will include other

Giovanni Bellini, *Madonna and Child Enthroned with
Saints* (1505). Saint Zaccaria, Venice. Photo courtesy
Cameraphoto Arte, Venice / Art Resource, NY.

murders (mostly not by Gabriel) and an attempt on the Pope's life, which Gabriel will foil. Our archangel gets cleaner, at least for a while.

So now let us find *him* in the process of cleaning/restoring *The Virgin and Child* in the church of San Zaccaria. Gabriel is up on a scaffold concealed from public view by a shroud and meditating on his work:

> *The restorer never tired of looking at it. He marveled at Bellini's skillful use of light and space, the powerful pulling that drew his eye inward and upward, the sculptural dignity of the Madonna and child and the saints surrounding them. It was a painting of utter silence. Even after a long, tedious morning of work, the painting blanketed him with a sense of peace* (p. 30).

This painting is classified by art historians as a *sacra conversazione*, a genre much in favor in religious art of the early sixteenth century. In this genre, as used in altarpieces, figures who attend *The Virgin and Child* share the same pictorial space with her and the infant, whereas in earlier altarpieces, each saint or dignitary occupied a separate panel. No representation of conversation takes place. Indeed, in the San Zaccaria altarpiece, despite the formal rearrangement, the figures are not only silent but also utterly still. They are locked in an interior space, except for the little angel in the center foreground who looks at us as she plays her instrument. Nobody else meets our eyes. The infant perhaps just raises his hand in blessing but does not smile. Gabriel understood this completely.

But what is a Jew doing restoring Roman Catholic images? The asymmetry here is remarked by Shamron, who reappears to summon Gabriel away from aesthetic peace to investigate Benjamin Stern's death: "I would love to see the look on the patriarch's face (Saint Zachary) if he ever found out that his precious altarpiece was being restored by a nice Jewish boy from the Jezreel valley" (p. 38). Saint Zachary, an old priest, was supposed to have been the father of St. John the Baptist. His wife was much too old for childbearing, but in the temple, the Archangel Gabriel appeared and told Zachary they would have a son. Incredulous, hence not full enough of faith, Zachary was struck mute. The legend tells that when the boy was born, Zachary recovered his speech. It is important to note that after his adventures in uncovering the evils of the reign of Pope Pius XII, Gabriel returned to the altarpiece and finished the restoration. But he also anonymously, in the brief last chapter, avenged his friend Benjamin Stern by putting an end to the career of The Leopard in the snow outside his Swiss chalet, two very different kinds of closure that pull in opposite directions on the ethical scale.

But all this is peripheral to the main story, which concerns the book that Benjamin Stern had written on the Wannsee Conference, already published, a bestseller, as mentioned on page 5. But now he is working on a new book; much of the material that he had been researching is still in his possession, promising a future revelation. It was this that led to his murder. What was the Wannsee Conference? Something vile that really happened. According to an article issued by the United States Holocaust Museum, "Wannsee Conference and the 'Final Solution,'" in January 20, 1942, fifteen high-ranking Nazi Party and German government officials gathered at a villa in the Berlin suburb of Wannsee to discuss how to implement Hitler's plan for the systematic annihilation of the Jews of Europe. Present were Reinhard Heydrich, Heinrich Muller, Adolf Eichmann, and, among the other twelve, Martin Luther, undersecretary of state.

It is surely no coincidence that in 2002, a year before *The Confessor*, there appeared a book titled *The Wannsee Conference and the Final Solution*. Its author was Paul Roseman, who happily is not dead but a specialist in Holocaust history and teaching at Indiana University. He is not listed, however, in the roster of sources to which Silva declares gratitude at the end of the novel. It is no risky guess that this book inspired *The Confessor*. Probably, Silva read the book and then used it as the historical starting point of his next fictional adventure. Martin Luther, a name of absurd historical ironies, is named in *The Confessor* as present at a fictional meeting at the convent in Brenzone supposedly witnessed by a young nun, who later reveals its dark secret. This meeting was between the Vatican Secretariat of State and three Germans, of whom Martin Luther was the leader and spokesman. This meeting "took place" in March 1942, that is, shortly after the actual Wannsee Conference, and was designed to assure at least the silence, if not the complicity, of the papacy in the face of the Final Solution. One of Luther's more vicious arguments was that the Holocaust would prevent the creation of a Jewish national state in Palestine:

> *If they have their own state, they would have the right, as the Vatican does, to send their diplomats round the world.*

Judaism, the ancient enemy of the Church, would be placed on the same footing as the Holy See. The Jewish state would become a platform for global Jewish domination (p. 287).

It turns out that Bishop Lorenzi, chief spokesman for the then Pope, Pius XII, is a member of the secret society Crux Vera, a right-wing group inside the Church, ultraconservative and already friendly to Germany. He quickly signs on to this agenda. After sixty years, Crux Vera killed Benjamin Stern through an assassin, an assassin who speaks Church Latin, to prevent that long and fiercely kept secret from sliming out of its hole. As with the secret Council of Rütli, this group has no historical footprint. Its very secretive nature would have prevented its being documented outside this novel, and perhaps it never existed.

The last third of *The Confessor* is dedicated to the meetings between Gabriel and Fr. Luigi Donati, the Pope's secretary, who would quickly become Gabriel's friend and, in later novels, enabler, as well as to the meeting between Gabriel and the Pope himself. Gabriel is pretty sure that the plan of Crux Vera includes the assassination of the Pope by Lange, and between them, they set up an effective defense. The novel's ideological climax takes place in the great Rome synagogue, where the new, best, imaginary pope plans to confess the role of the papacy in failing to confront and defend the Jews as they were rounded up in the autumn of 1943 and carted away beneath the Vatican windows. His speech is explicitly offered as a confession, an atonement, preparatory to a still greater confession that will be possible when *all* the secret documents of the Vatican shall be laid open to public scrutiny as this pope promises they shall be. The "Author's Note" at the end of the novel remarks wearily that this has not yet happened, blocked at the end of the century by the new, real, Vatican Secretary of State, Cardinal Sodano:

Cardinal Sodano, it was suggested, opposes opening the Archives because it would set a terribly dangerous precedent and leave the Vatican vulnerable to other historical investigations, such as the relationship between the Holy See and the murderous regimes of Latin America (p. 455).

There is still one more confession and request for absolution to come, but it would spoil the plot if I were to reveal it. Since this returns us to ethical issues, I must note that by the end of this novel, Gabriel is not so clean. He has personally killed some anonymous Italian policemen and Lange's female accomplice, Katrine. Of course, he suffers the retribution of extreme damage to himself in the final chase (atonement?) and then, when having recovered in the Pope's own hospital wing, returns to his Bellini as aesthetic absolution. Yet at the very end, he tracks down Lange and kills him in revenge for the murder of Benjamin Stern. So we are back where we were in *The Kill Artist*, seeking clarity about when, if ever, violent killing is, if not acceptable, excusable.

A Death In Vienna

This third Holocaust novel appears under a title that seems to return Gabriel Allon to 1991, witnessing the horrifying death of his son in a street in Vienna, where his car has been bombed by Tariq. But not so. It is 2004, that is, "more than three years" (p. 117) after *The Kill Artist* that had featured Gabriel's revenge for that atrocity, which itself was "thirteen years" ago (p. 32). This kind of interior dating is one of the tools that Silva uses to make the reader work. Gabriel is not, in fact, in Vienna when the book opens but in Venice, where he is restoring another great Bellini altarpiece, the *Saints Christopher, Jerome, and Louis of Toulouse* in the church of San Giovanni Crisostomo. Still there for our viewing, perhaps we have Gabriel to thank for its excellent condition.

This altarpiece, the last that Bellini executed in his old age in 1513, is as different as it could possibly be from the San Zaccaria *sacra conversazione*, although, obviously, it was itself in conversation with that earlier triumph. First, it omits *The Virgin and Child* as the pinnacle of the composition, their place being taken by St. Jerome, in whom Bellini was deeply interested (he also appears frontally in the San Zaccaria image deep in a book of Psalms). All the figures are richly humanized. Both St. Christopher and St. Louis appear to look at the lookers; and the child on the back of St. Christopher, as in the legend where the saint-to-be carries him across the river, is sucking his thumb. St. Jerome is reading as usual, but his pose is relaxed in three-quarter view (unusual for an altarpiece); and he is half *en plein air*, being himself the apex of a landscape, with a fig tree and a river behind him. The wooden staff of the workman and the crozier of the churchman, carefully matched in position and length, might seem, if not to support St.

Giovanni Bellini, *Saints Christopher, Jerome, and Louis of Toulouse* (1513). San Giovanni Crisostomo Altarpiece, Venice. Photo courtesy Cameraphoto Arte, Venice / Art Resource, NY.

Jerome, at least be ready to prevent him from slipping off his rock. At the end of his career, Bellini was stating his independence from tradition and perhaps even from parts of Catholic belief.

Here is Gabriel's own response to the painting. It "glowed." St. Louis is "draped in a cape of red and gold brocade," St. Jerome is "framed by a vibrant blue sky streaked with gray-brown clouds," St. Christopher is draped in a "rose-colored tunic," yet "each saint was separated from the other, alone before God, the isolation so complete it was almost painful to observe" (p. 12–13). This is a painterly response based on color rather than iconography, but it enables him to win an argument with another restorer, Van Marle, who had tried to attribute the richness of color to collaboration between Bellini and Titian. Raimond van Marle was a real art historian who died in 1936, his magnum opus incomplete. It gives us a sense of how much research went into a Silva novel. And as before, Gabriel returns at the end of the novel to finish his restoration of the altarpiece, not quite at the end to be truthful. He still has an act of vengeance to accomplish.

So we begin the novel by better understanding Gabriel's status as a restorer, something that lends him too color and depth; but you will be asking, what about the story? Well, there is a connection between this graceful opening and the main plot, which involves Gabriel's mother, who survived the Holocaust by sheer grit and courage and arrived in Israel. When his mother, Irene, arrived in Israel, she had endured weeks of torture at Birkenau, torture by near starvation and heavy work, culminating in the notorious Death March away from the camp so that the arriving allies would not discover its true business. By chance, she was pulled from the march by the man who will become the chief object of Gabriel's other skills, Erich Radek, a German Sturmbannführer who had been sent to clean up the evidence of German atrocities. Testing her to see if she will become evidence for the prosecution later, he fixes his face forever in her memory; and when she returns to Israel, she too becomes a painter. Among many images of Birkenau, she paints the figure of Radek all in black, which will allow Gabriel to identify him with certainty long after his mother has died. Later, he is given her own written account of the Death March, a testimony parallel to that of Sister Regina's in *The Confessor* in that its "documentary" status helps to enlist readerly belief.

Erich Radek was not a historical person though he is clearly and admittedly a stand-in for Paul Blobel, to whom Eichmann assigned the task of getting rid of the thousands of Jewish corpses that had been unsatisfactorily buried outside many of the concentration camps and were starting to bubble and smell. Silva here invokes the historical fact of Action 1005, the assignment given to Blobel (pp. 134–135). Blobel was hanged in Landsberg Prison in 1951. His fictional avatar, Radek, however, escaped completely, having worked for the American CIA in the immediate aftermath of World War II and disappearing behind a pseudonym Ludwig Vogel, which allows him to live peacefully in Zurich. There, drawing on the immense wealth he has stored in Swiss banks, he can be found calmly drinking coffee at the Café Central. Someone, Max Klein, who has known him at Auschwitz, recognizes him by his voice and alerts Eli Lavon, who runs an office dealing with "Wartime Claims and Inquiries." It scarcely needs saying that Max Klein is murdered, and Lavon's office is bombed, killing his two young secretaries and putting Lavon himself in hospital, very likely to die. It is the news of Lavon's near assassination that, in the first place, leads Shamron to track down Gabriel at work on his Bellini and send him out again to discover who was responsible, the first hypothesis being that it was Islamic terrorists.

The chief reason for Radek's hiding, even if in plain sight, is that his son, Peter Metzler, is currently running for the position of Chancellor in the Austrian state as a far-right candidate. Radek/Vogel believes that discovery of his patronage and the source of his funding would cost his son the election. I have already given away more of the plot than is wise, but perhaps it is necessary since this is one of the most complicated plots in all of the Silva novels, including a false trail following a person assumed to be Radek to Argentina. The only value of this plot—and false trails tend to annoy readers—is to bring in once again the activities of the Vatican in shielding and transferring Nazis out of Europe into more sympathetic regimes, of which Argentina was a notorious example. The chief culprit here was a historical figure, Bishop Alois Hudal, a complex figure with a complex biography, who died in 1963 but who is perhaps best known and reviled for his 1937 book, *The Foundations of National Socialism*. He became bishop of the congregation of Santa Maria dell'Anima in Rome, appointed by Pope Pius XI to keep the Anima in Austrian rather than German hands. The book, however, ruined his relationship with the papacy; and he was forced to resign from the Anima in 1952. In the interim, however, he had gained notoriety by helping to create the Ratlines, helping former

Nazis, including war criminals, to escape Germany as the war came to an end and find safe haven in Latin America, especially Argentina. To what extent Pope Pius XI was complicit in this operation is not clear, but he surely knew about it.

This chunk of Holocaust history lends a kind of grandeur to the novel and shifts the onus, if not the blame, from Blobel/Radek/Vogel to the criminal institutions he served. One of these was, believe it or not, the CIA, a shabby story elicited from Adrian Carter, the American espiocrat, with whom Gabriel had already had had dealings, with many more to come. The story Carter told was about the very beginning of the Cold War when America was desperate for information about its new foe, Soviet Russia, and how into their arms had fallen Gen. Reinhard Gehlen, who had already spent years spying on the Russians. Gehlen wanted Radek as his assistant, and so he was released from internment at Mannheim to enter the service of the CIA. I will leave Adrian Carter to tell the rest of the shameful story about how the Americans helped Radek stay under the radar when the Nuremberg trials were in process and thereafter. "We cleaned up the files in the Staatsarchiv. We created a company for him to run, Danube Valley Trade and Investment . . . Before long, profits from DVTI were funding all of our Austrian nets. In short, Vogel was our most important asset in Austria . . . He was a master spy. When the Wall came down, his work was done" (p. 287).

When Radek/Vogel is firmly identified by the Israelis, the punishment for his part in Action 1005 is not death but capture—kidnapping—and imprisonment in Israel, much as Eichmann had been daringly snatched by Shamron, an episode which Shamron is never hesitant to retell. Unlike Eichmann, however, Radek's capture does not lead to his execution but to an exercise comparable to confession but without atonement. Radek's transfer to Israel is interrupted by a forced return to Treblinka, wherein the reader receives a mental tour of the camp with Radek as tour director. In prison in Israel, he is forced to reveal to Israeli historians his responsibility for Action 1005 as well as the Death March and murders around it. Unlike confession, however, Radek's account of his behavior is totally without remorse. As it turns out, the news of his capture has no effect on the Austrian election, and his right-wing son is returned with a clear majority. The novel is thus depressingly open-ended, except for the CIA's forced return of Radek's two and a half billion dollars extracted by blackmail from

Carter by Shamron, who realized that the agency would pay up to avoid exposure of its shameful role in the affair. As Carter says, if "you expose the fact the Radek was our man in Vienna it will cause the Agency much public embarrassment at a time when it is locked in a global campaign against forces that wish to destroy my country *and* yours" (p. 289–290). The money, of course, went back to Israel.

Something must be said about Austrian politics, which Silva touches only lightly in the novel while reminding us in his "Author's Note" of the career of Jorg Haider (p. 419). This tip encourages the reader to remember a period in the modern history of Austria when Haider rose to prominence as leader of the Austrian Freedom Party (FPO), which accumulated many far-right members. Haider himself made statements that endorsed the German military, once called the concentration camps "punishment camps," was known to have received a large sum of money from dealings with Gaddafi, and visited Saddam Hussein on the eve of the American invasion in 2003. The Israeli Mossad was keeping him closely under observation. *A Death in Vienna* appeared in 2004. There are no close parallels between Metzler and Haider; but the news coming out of Austria, if one were paying attention, suggested a political climate in which anti-Semitism was always on the verge, like the burying pits outside the camps, of bubbling to the surface.

This novel has a rather more intricate relationship to historical fact than the previous ones, as becomes the gravity of its subject. One need only probe a little to realize that the novel is doing moral work. It is, more than the first two in this series, a Holocaust memorial. Its concept of justice shows how deeply Silva is investigating the paradox of the assassin, especially one who kills on the orders of a state. And here, it gets *really* interesting. Before beginning his kidnapping operation, Gabriel has to run it by the Israeli prime minister. The real prime minister at the time of the novel's writing and publication was Ariel Sharon, the chief hawk and perhaps war criminal who is surely the model for Shamron. How weird is that? It is clear from the interview that "Ariel Sharon" would be quite content to have Gabriel put "Radek down and have the dogs lick his blood," a reference to I Kings 21:19. "Hast thou killed and taken possession . . . Thus saith the Lord, In the place where dogs licked the blood of Naboth shall dogs lick thy blood, even thine." Silva will return to this quotation in his next novel, where "taking possession" is a central theme. But Gabriel's position is different. "I don't want to kill an old man" (p. 337). "I know he's a monster. I just don't want to kill him. I want the world to know what this man did" (p. 337).

Silva's "Author's Note" to the novel is more explicit on which parts are fiction and which parts are clearly historical. But he does not explain the value of this method. It allows him to have it both ways. "Based loosely on actual events," the novel (and the note) not only encourages our self-education but also implicitly raises the question of what, in historical accounts of the past where huge interests are still at stake, "actual events" may still be partly fiction, influenced by who exactly is telling the story. There are, of course, still the Holocaust deniers; and in response to them, first-person testimony, such as that of Gabriel's mother, even though fictional, may work better than insulting them. Taking the reader on a tour of Treblinka is also powerfully persuasive, not least because so little remains. But in subsequent novels, we will learn more about the CIA and its absolute reliance on deception, another form of self-education that Americans should frequently indulge in.

THE PRINCE OF FIRE

Silva didn't wait or make Gabriel wait before setting up his next adventure, which once again focuses on Israel and Palestine (and Libya) and their tortured embrace. On page 41, Gabriel reverts, if only in his mind, to the fact that "two months previously he had engineered the capture of an Austrian war criminal named Erich Radek and returned him to Israel to face justice." There is a dreadful irony in the fact that this thought occurs in the presence of his wrecked wife, Leah, around whose clever capture from her English nursing home this new plot will develop. "He likes his women damaged," indeed. The year is now 2005. And "two years earlier he had saved the pope's life" (p. 55). The internal or sequential chronology is important to Silva, keeping the sequence tightly linked and always up to the minute. But this novel insists talking about the past, the Israeli past, in a series of conversations that involve us in soul-searching as to whether the endless crises caused by the founding of the state of Israel could have been avoided.

The *Prince of Fire* is an honorific bestowed upon Gabriel by Shamron, previously mentioned in *A Death in Vienna* (p. 308). It serves to remind the reader that Gabriel is something almost unworldly in the world of espionage and assassination, an archangel. Behind him lurks the Red Prince, a real person on the opposite side. Ali Hassan Salameh, code name Abu Hassan, was the leader of Black September and responsible for the 1972 Munich massacre. His nickname was the Red Prince, a sign of his popularity, and he had secret links to the CIA. He was assassinated by the Israeli Mossad in 1979. This allusion to Salameh, confirmed in the "Author's Notes," serves to further complicate Silva's relationship to the Israel/Palestine problem. They are two sides of the same coin. This novel will give more credence and sympathy to the Palestinians than any of the previous ones; and it achieves this by stories within the main story, interpolated narratives from the past, as well as by debates between Gabriel and Shamron.

The novel opens with a blast. The Israeli embassy in Rome is shattered by a car bomb, actually, a large truck loaded with explosives that comes barreling down a quiet street, followed by a dark car with heavily armed men to cut down any survivors. Among the victims was "an Italian couple, sickened by the new rise of European anti-Semitism, who were about to inquire about the possibility of emigrating to Israel" (p. 8). Unspoken ironies are among Silva's specialties.

Paintings: because Gabriel has been summoned back to Israel to protect him against the terrorists' possession of a complete dossier on him, he cannot finish restoring the second Bellini. He hands it over to his own teacher, Tiepolo. Prior to this, however, he has half committed himself to restoring a Rubens for our friend Julian Isherwood for the princely sum of two hundred thousand pounds. A very dirty painting, it had been attributed to Erasmus Quellinus, but Gabriel knows better. Better still, its subject was *Daniel in the Lions' Den*, another Daniel, rescued not by an angel but by human art. In chapter 37, Gabriel is back at work restoring the Rubens in his apartment in Tel Aviv with the rescued Leah watching. It goes without saying that the story of how Isherwood acquired the painting "from a draughty Georgian pile in the Cotswolds" is entirely fictional. In reality, it has one of the most complete and aristocratic provenances in art history and was bought by the National Gallery of Art in Washington, D.C., in December 1965. If we wish to consider the iconography, it is hard to tell human fear from earnest prayer; but the subject of imprisonment among metaphorical beasts is one that Silva will explore in several more novels, usually with a woman in Daniel's position. In this painting (as also in Rembrandt's drawing of the same scene), the lions are charmingly (because charmed) unthreatening.

This novel takes upon itself the task of explaining to readers around the world what happened in the Middle East in the past to create the endless, rebarbative, unjustifiable violence of the very present. It takes it upon itself not to justify the Israeli/Zionist position but to place it in direct juxtaposition to the Arab/Palestinian position. We have to read the novel

Peter Paul Rubens, *Daniel in the Lions' Den* (c. 1614/1616). National Gallery of Art, Washington. Aisla Mellon Bruce Fund 1965.13.1.

to adjudicate between them or fail to. It turns out that the bombing of the Israeli embassy is not a chance choice but a (very wasteful) move to draw Gabriel out of his painter's lair. One of the assassins, Douad Hadawi, was discovered to have a videotape of Gabriel's dossier, covering his whole career so far and clearly marking him out as an important target for the future. So rather than wait for the enemy to come to the gates of Tel Aviv, Gabriel is sent out to track down the mastermind behind the spectacularly staged and politically pointed violence. For this, he has help, another damaged woman, an Israeli who lost her mother and two sisters to a bombing of a bus in Tel Aviv and who walked thereafter with a limp. Dina has a theory, which grows out of a photograph of a young boy sitting in the lap of "a distraught older man: Yasir Arafat" (72). The child is Khaled al-Khalifa. The occasion is the funeral of his father, Sabri al-Khalifa. Another photograph shows Asad al-Khalifa, Khaled's grandfather. "And the story begins with him" (p. 73). So claims Dina, the narrator, and offers up a long tale, which will point to the mysterious Khaled as the perpetrator.

The story includes the Arab Revolt of 1936–1939 and its collapse in fighting among warlords; the role of Sheikh Assad, a man "with the courage of a lion," (p. 77) as the formidable new leader of the Arab military resistance; the partitioning of the land by the British in 1947; Assad's assassination by Ari Shamron in 1948 at the bidding of Yitzhak Rabin, the Israeli president at the time; the Six Days War of 1967, the worst possible setback for the Arab cause; and the enrolment of Assad's son, Sabri al-Khalifa, by Yasir Arafat, who had him tutored in the craft of terrorism. At the top of Sabri's achievements was the 1972 Munich massacre, which in turn was followed, as we already know, by Gabriel's killing of Sabri, ordered by Prime Minister Golda Meir, whose orders were transmitted by Shamron. This tale includes many conversations that Dina has imagined though the events at their heart were "true." Thus, the story comes full circle. From this dire sequence of events, Dina has inferred that Khaled, who had been adopted by Arafat but has since vanished from sight, was now continuing the cycle of vengeance. As proof of this conjecture, she takes them to visit the ruins of Beit Sayeed (an Arab village that never existed and could therefore not have been destroyed) and adds an improbable link to Douad Hassawi, whose grandfather was killed there by Shamron in his raid on Sheikh Assad. The broader message is that in the Middle East family ties and clans are more important than politics, reminding us that that is how vendettas usually work.

What increases our instinctive suspicion of Dina's narrative is that she sets up a new tool for the Israelis' intelligence system—symbolic dating. She notes that new attacks tend to occur on the same day or even at the same time (allowing for time differences) as Israeli attacks, therefore increasing the "eye for an eye" scenario. Once grasped, this principle gives the Israelis something like advance but highly selective knowledge of what is going to happen. Somewhere at 7:00 p.m. precisely, on April 18, 2004, anniversary of the demolition of the fabled Beit Sayeed in 1948, fifty-six years earlier, there will be another horrific terrorist attack. But where? And why choose 2004 as your year of reprisal? Also, advance knowledge, if that is what it is, doesn't work very well as a preventative, as this novel will demonstrate.

Something small is, however, worth noting. When Shamron reports back to Rabin that he has successfully taken out Asad al-Khalifa, Rabin is quoted as saying, "Good. Let the dogs lap up his blood." How Dina is supposed to have been privy to the conversation is not explained. But the quotation from I Kings 21:17–19 is rebarbative. It is part of the rebuke that the prophet Elijah gives the tyrant Ahab for arranging the murder of Nathan the Jezreelite in order to acquire the vineyard that Nathan refused to sell him: "Thus says the Lord: Have you killed, and also taken possession . . . In the place where dogs licked up the blood of Naboth, dogs will also lick up your blood." We have heard this quotation before in *A Death in Vienna* (p. 308) without the allegorical significance here since it applied only to Radek. The obvious candidate for the role of Ahab is Israel and its leaders. In his "Author's Note," Silva remarks that no such village as Beit Sayeed ever existed; but he adds, "There once was a village called Sumayriyya in western Galilee. Its destruction occurred as described [here]." The Israeli plan for "taking possession" of Arab lands and villages was indeed called Tochnit Dalet (Plan D). Even a not very enterprising reader can find a great deal of troubling information online about Tochnit Dalet, including claims that it was intended as ethnic cleansing. And the emotional importance of Sumayriyya to this narrative is undeniable.

This is the first Silva novel to take account of the Separation Fence, Israel's second answer to the problems of taking possession, the first being military force. And this too is riven with ambivalence. When Yonatan, a colonel in the Israeli army who is also Shamron's son, accompanies Gabriel to a meeting with Arafat, he asks Gabriel what he thinks of the Wall. And when Gabriel replies equivocally, "It's certainly nothing to be proud of," Yonatan, who is alienated from his father, gives an equivocal defense:

I think it's an ugly scar across this beautiful land of ours. It's our new Wailing Wall, much longer than the first, and different because now people are wailing on both sides of the wall. But I'm afraid we have no other choice. With good intelligence we've managed to stop most of the suicide attacks, but we'll never be able to stop them all. We need this fence (p. 133).

"But," responds Gabriel, "it's not the only reason we're building it." "That's true," Yonatan said. "When it's finished, it will allow us to turn our backs on the Arabs and walk away. That's why they're so afraid of it. It's in their interest to remain chained to us in conflict."

Where is Silva's voice in this exchange? Is Yonatan's interpretation correct? Gabriel's serves only to open a question that may not be adequately answered here, although it does require us to add information about the Wall and its critics. The security argument made by Yonatan *has* been justified by the significant reduction in the number of suicide attacks since the Wall was built, yet it remains in defiance of international law and is rightfully suspected of being a device to enlarge Israeli territory not only by taking Palestinian land for the wall's construction but also by embracing more than fifty illegal settlements. The land taken is some of the most fertile in the region. The restraints that the Wall has placed on Palestinians wishing to work in Israel or farm their own lands are such that, in the views of critics, it will only breed further outrage among the Palestinians and lead ultimately to more violence. Access to hospitals and to water has been seriously affected. In July 2004, the United Nations accepted Resolution ES-10/15, condemning the barrier; and Israel was joined in its rejection of the resolution by, of course, the United States. There were 150 countries that voted in favor, including all 25 members of the European Union. Alas, it has become a fait accompli, creating in effect a new boundary much to the advantage of Israel and a sign of the weakness of international law.

But any ambivalence about Palestine and its leader, Yasir Arafat, evaporates in the next scene, where Gabriel confronts the old man himself. "For thirty years they had been swimming together in the same river of blood" (p. 140), but Gabriel refuses to see them as fated adversaries, noting Arafat's professions of interest in peace are vitiated by his refusal of the generous deal offered to him by President Bill Clinton at Camp David in 1978. Their conversation is a barbed draw. Arafat refuses to admit that there is such a man as Khaled, still less, of course, that he himself deploys him as a terrorist. At the end of the novel, Silva remarks in his "Author's Note" that Arafat fell ill and died as he "was completing this novel. Had he chosen the path of peace instead of unleashing a wave of terror, it would have never been written" (p. 405). By demonizing Arafat here, especially after the rather sympathetic portrait of him in *The Killer Artist*, Silva cuts short the debate that he seems to have started. And it will have to be taken up by Yonatan's informer, who for the price of his wife's treatment for cancer in a Jerusalem hospital is capable of betraying Arafat, revealing that Khaled does indeed exist and even supplies a photograph of him, to be compared, for better identification, with the image of a child on Arafat's lap. And the informer states, as critics of the Wall sometimes do, that with the Wall Israel is building "the first Palestinian Ghetto." "Worse still, you're building a ghetto for yourselves" (p. 160). Given demographics, this dark prophecy is more likely than not to be fulfilled.

The next section of the novel has an entirely different tone. We are out of the shadow of the Wall, in "Paris by the Nile," that is, Cairo, to which Gabriel has come on the trail of Khaled; and we are even allowed a dash of humor in the comic battle between Gabriel's new persona, the hypercritical Herr Klemp, and Mr. Katubi, the chief concierge at Gabriel's hotel. Here, we do return to the espionage novel with all its tricks—illegal entry, the placing of a "glass" on the phone of the mysterious Mimi (a vamp out of the 1930s), and endless surveillance of the apartment in which Khaled is occasionally to be found. Here also comes comedy. Gabriel will encounter "an angora cat with a weight problem" (p. 187) and a Nubian doorman who has to be lured away for a short while. We have entered, for a space, the territory of the caper movie. "The cat looked at Gabriel without interest, then rested its chin on its paws and closed its eyes" (p. 191). You can see that cat, considerably enlarged, at the feet of *Daniel in the Lions' Den* as imagined by Rubens. Then Silva turns to open farce, having Herr Klemp, needing to stay in his hotel for several more days, take by mouth a remedy for constipation that is properly administered anally. The bodily results are catastrophic.

The tone is a welcome break for the catastrophe of quite another nature to which the whole plot has been tending. For obvious reasons, I cannot reveal what this is, or what role Gabriel played in it, or his reason for being on the spot. What I do want to focus on may seem to the reader a tiresome, suspense-building digression, an interpolated narrative, delivered to Gabriel by an enflamed young Palestinian woman. Concealing her real name, she allows Gabriel to call her Palestina, thereby creating allegory; and she comes from Sumayriyya (little Samaria), that is, a real Arab village, now eradicated. Her story is brilliantly told:

Sumayriyya? . . . It was Paradise on Earth. Eden. Fruit orchards and olive groves. Melons and bananas, cucumbers and wheat. Sumayriyya was simple. Pure. Our life moved to the rhythms of the planting and the harvest. The rains and the drought. We were eight hundred in Sumayriyya. We had a mosque. We had a school. We were poor, but Allah blessed us with everything we needed.

On the night of May 13, 1948, a column of armored Haganah vehicles set out up the coast road from Acre. Their action was code-named Operation Ben-Ami. It was part of Tochnit Dalet . . . The stated objection of Operation Ben-Ami was the reinforcement of several isolated Jewish settlements in the Western Galilee. The real objective, however, was conquest and annexation. In fact, the orders specifically called for the destruction of three Arab villages: Bass, Zib, and Sumayriyya.

All three villages like Acre and Haifa were on the coast, which the Israelis needed for access to the sea.

Sumayriyya was the first of the villages to die (continued Palestina) . . . The Jews wanted us to leave. They intentionally left the eastern side of the village unguarded to give us an escape route. We had no time to pack anything or even to take something to eat . . . The Jews told us to go to Lebanon . . . So we kept walking. We walked over the border, into exile. Into oblivion. And behind us the gates of Palestine were being forever barred against our return . . . In June Ben Gurion said that the refugees could not come home . . . We would be a thorn in the side of the new Jewish state. We knew then that we would never see Sumayriyya again. Paradise Lost (pp. 295–299).

Unlike the exile described in Genesis and redescribed by John Milton, the title of whose great poem is Palestina's final phrase here, this was no myth but attested history, which, of course, had acquired mythical status in the Arab imagination. The assault on the village during Operation Ben-Ami was one day prior to the official outbreak of the 1948 Arab-Israeli war, which from Gabriel's perspective in 2005 had a strong claim to be the originating cause of the endless war in which he was now trapped.

As before, I shall keep mum on what that was, for you must continue reading until the very end when, after the catastrophe, Gabriel actually discovers Khaled engaged in *his* other profession, working as an archeologist of stature. The two enemies share the patience and the values of the artist/restorer. In fact, there was a Khaled Assad, Syrian archeologist and head of antiquities for the ancient city of Palmyra, Syria, a UNESCO World Heritage site. He was killed by Isis in 2015. But his fictional avatar is killed by Gabriel in 2005. In his trench in a dig in France, "Paul Martineau" is challenged by Gabriel to speak his real name. "You are Khaled, son of Sabri, Grandson of Asad, the Lion of Beit Sayeed." Then he shoots him. So much for the lion.

And Gabriel has already returned to his work on *Daniel in the Lions' Den*, the tedious task of scrubbing more than a century's worth of dirt and grime "from the surface of the painting" (p. 397).

EGYPT AND
SAUDI ARABIA

THE MESSENGER

This novel, the fifth in the Gabriel Allon collection, looking solely at publication order, initiates another series within a series to follow the Holocaust group, which Silva had announced only as it reached its conclusion. I call this group the Saudi series though its focus on Saudi Arabia develops slowly and eventually includes the whole Middle East region, whose largest, most powerful, and most problematic member is Saudi Arabia itself. The group includes *The Messenger* (2006–2007), *The Secret Servant* (2007–2008), and as a considerable afterthought, *Portrait of a Spy* (2011). It is important to notice when the books were published because one of the dangers of relevance—writing to the minute—is that the minute passes. As real events move on, their fictional equivalents may become out of date. Readers must do the updating themselves, charitably.

The Messenger demonstrates the silky perfection with which Daniel Silva intersects and interrelates different themes and story lines. It opens with Gabriel as the man of restoration, peacefully finishing up his work on Rubens' *Daniel in the Lion's Den*, followed by dramatic shock: an enormously successful terrorist attack on our favorite pope, who survives, thanks to Gabriel. The next stage is the identification of the perpetrators and the discovery that they are funded by Saudi Arabia. The immediate architect of the attack on the pope is Ahmed bin Shafik, a former member of the Saudi intelligence service, who has now "gone into private practice" (p. 125). Behind him lies Prince Nabil, the Saudi interior minister, whom the Israelis call the Prince of Darkness. But now Silva allows Gabriel to reunite with his lover, Chiara, who had left him because of his inability to legally sever himself from his hopelessly damaged wife. We go from darkness to light, from tragedy to romance, in the change of chapters. Then we reenter the labyrinth politics of the CIA, whose director, Adrian Carter, wants to "outsource" the killing of Bin Shafik to the Israelis, creating deniability for the American government, which is up to its neck in Saudi money. Bin Shafik is protected by the Saudi billionaire Zizi al-Bakari, and Gabriel needs to penetrate that pearly shell. This theme, countering Al-Qaeda and its offshoots, then merges with that of resurgent anti-Semitism in Europe, particularly in France. A Jewish woman, Hannah Weinberg, who is formally protesting anti-Semitism in Paris, also happens to be the possessor of a fabled Van Gogh portrait, which will be used as a tool in the trap to be set for Zizi.

The novel sets itself carefully in 2006, the year of its actual publication. We are three years after *The Confessor* (2003), two years after *A Death in Vienna* (2004) (pp. 27–28), and six months after *Prince of Fire* (p. 20). Time is hastening. The American president at this time is clearly George Bush, indirectly named via a road sign (GEORGE BUSH CENTER FOR INTELLIGENCE), probably not at this time ironic. His visit to the Vatican toward the end of the novel, and the terrorist attack there on his life, has no basis in fact. Bush did visit the Vatican in June 2004, uneventfully. The Israeli prime minister, who is never named, must be Ariel Sharon, of whom we have previously learned disturbing things; and he is ruthless in his decree that Bin Shafik must be exterminated. The French President, who is reported to have announced that there is "no anti-Semitism in France" (p. 195), is Jacques Chiraq. The new recruit to Carter and Gabriel's team is Sarah Bancroft, whose fiancé was killed in 2001 when his plane was flown into one of the Twin Towers. It is now well known that thirteen of the Twin Towers terrorists were Saudi Arabians. As of this writing, the bereaved are prevented from suing the Saudi government by an American law that gives foreign governments immunity.

Silva is keeping a lot of big political balls in the air at once as well as increasing the number of persons we care about. Sarah will feature in two more novels, creating another form of linkage to compare with that of the pope, as also very slight sexual tension since she immediately falls in love with Gabriel. Because of his carelessness, she is captured and tortured but, of course, since this is fiction, rescued by Gabriel and his team. This rescue involves the killing of an entire terrorist cell, eleven men, a slaughter, very different from the one-on-one assassination in which Gabriel more honorably specializes though it is presumably justified by what was done to Sarah. She is the titular Messenger (p. 444), and when she recovers, she will return to the CIA at the Saudi desk.

After the second attack on the Vatican near the end of the novel, in which Gabriel's friend Monsignor Donati throws himself in front of the American President as a shield, Gabriel is summoned to testify before a Senate committee in Washington to explain "how the forces of global Islamic terrorism had managed to penetrate the center of Christendom" (p. 462). He uses the opportunity well. "The senators need to know about the true nature of the Saudi regime and its support for global terrorism. The American people need to know how all those petrodollars are being spent" (p. 463). Suffice it to say that the hunt for Ahmed bin Shafiq comes to its only possible conclusion; and Zizi al-Bakari, his patron, is also eliminated in the streets of Cannes, a closing that is merely a reopening, "for the last thing . . . seen . . . was Nadia al-Bakari, kneeling over the dead body of her father, screaming for revenge" (p. 485). This, we will discover some years later, points forward to *Portrait of a Spy*, in which Saudi power and influence is the major theme; and Nadia joins the side of the angels.

But if you are already growing tired of revenge, take a break, a break that Silva himself has provided, by visiting that part of the plot of *The Messenger* that deals with the painting used to lure Zizi al-Bakari to the art dealership of Julian Isherwood. Gabriel has learned that Zizi, among his other financial exploits, is a major art collector and does not own a Van Gogh. "He's dropped hints from time to time that's he's looking for one. And not just any van Gogh. He wants something special" (p 173). This digression—for it completely changes our reading experience—begins in the genre of comedy: "I need a Van Gogh, Julian," [says Gabriel]. "Don't we all, petal," replies Julian Isherwood, using his favorite pet name for Gabriel (p. 159). Under interrogation by Gabriel, Isherwood tells a story about an unknown (and imaginary) portrait by Van Gogh, "Marguerite Gachet at her dressing table," which Isherwood had learned about in his father's diaries, belonging to a family named Weinberg and very, very definitely not for sale. Isherwood's story, however, quickly turns the genre from comedy to romantic tragedy as he recounts how Van Gogh, after his stay in a mental hospital, moves to Auvers-sur-Oise, a quiet country town about twenty miles outside Paris, and puts himself in the care of Dr. Paul Gachet. Gachet had a daughter, Marguerite, who, according to Isherwood, became infatuated with Van Gogh; and perhaps, though, Isherwood does not suggest this, it was mutual, for Van Gogh proceeded to paint several portraits of Marguerite, one in her garden, in a white dress that looks suspiciously like a wedding gown, and one at the piano, where after several sketches of her in pink and pale blue, she appears in a white gown with a rainbow sheen. There is also a *Girl in White* almost identical to Marguerite's appearance in her garden but with no garden, only stylized flowers in the background. And according to Isherwood (who does not mention this third portrait), she and Vincent appear together in *Undergrowth with Two Figures*, which Isherwood sees as Vincent and Marguerite walking toward us between an aisle of trees: "Vincent's premonition of marriage" (p. 165). They were all painted in 1890. This is where Isherwood (and Silva) abandons art history and engages in wishful thinking, describing a fourth painting, *Marguerite Gachet at Her Dressing Table*, "The pose and the setting are clearly representative of a bride on her wedding night," says Isherwood (p. 167), who has never seen it! But he speculates that it was this portrait, because of its intimacy, which *might* have caused a breach between Dr. Gachet and Van Gogh, and a veto on the relationship, which *might* in turn have precipitated the painter's clumsy suicide.

The painting never appears in the inventory of Van Gogh's paintings (not surprisingly, says the reader, since it was completely imaginary). In the invented part of the story, it disappeared into a private holding in the family of Hannah Weinberg, whom we met in the first paragraph of this chapter. When, with the help of Uzi Navot, Gabriel tracks her down, she provides a link back to Silva's Holocaust series since she was a witness in 1942 when her father removed the painting from its stretcher and hid it beneath the floorboards to protect it from the ravening Nazis. Now it hangs in her bedroom. So ravishing is this story in its interweaving of art history and romantic fiction that we *want* it to be true; we applaud Hannah Weinberg's willingness to "rent" the painting to Gabriel to become the bait in his trap for Zizi al-Bakari.

In the same vein, visitors to the National Gallery of Art in Washington, D.C., will be surprised to learn, at the beginning of chapter 18, that "Isherwood Fine Arts had sold *Daniel in the Lions' Den* by Peter Paul Rubens in the first Wednesday of the new year" (p. 229) since this would be in January 2006 (or perhaps 2005), whereas in fact, the painting has been hanging in the National Gallery since 1965. But it is nice to know that in the world of fiction, Julian Isherwood made a great deal of money on it—ten million pounds, less Gabriel's fee! This begins the theme of immense wealth that marks this novel—Saudi wealth, Zizi's personal wealth, the proposed rental fee for *Marguerite Gachet* (seventy-two million dollars), and the price Zizi paid for it (eighty-five million); some readers may feel themselves thoroughly outspent. But by now, such huge figures are in the news all the time, being the effect of the takeover of the finance industry by hedge fund managers. Incidentally, we are never told how Gabriel recovered *Marguerite* and returned her to Hannah Weinberg when, it had been agreed, she would return the money, keeping only the very substantial interest for use in her anti-Semitism campaign.

But the real moral center of the novel occurs early in the dialogue between Gabriel and Adrian Carter (rapidly becoming a fixture in Silva novels) about why the United States itself cannot or will not go after Zizi al-Bakari despite clear evidence that his money has been financing terrorism. "Why?" asks Gabriel.

Vincent van Gogh, *Mademoiselle Gachet at the Piano* (1890). Kunstmuseum Basel. Photo courtesy Bridgeman-Giraudon / Art Resource, NY.

"Money," *said Carter, then added, "And oil, of course." The Saudi Royal Family has a lot of friends in Washington—the kind of friends only money can buy . . . If Zizi's battalion of Washington Lawyers even suspected he was the target of a criminal probe, Zizi would call his Majesty, and his Majesty would call Ambassador Bashir, and Ambassador Bashir would pop over to the White House for a little chat with the president. He would remind the president that a twist or two on the oil spigots would send the price of gasoline over five dollars a gallon"* (p. 135).

This part of the argument is obviously obsolete now. Not only has oil been flowing so freely that prices have descended to levels disastrous to certain businesses (including the Soviet Union), but also the current American president, Barak Obama, on his last lap, has visited Saudi Arabia to raise issues unimaginable in 2006. But in 2006, it was possible to imagine that "Bush" has passed on a request to the Israelis to deal with Zizi themselves so that the United States "can maintain plausible deniability in Riyadh" (p. 137). Vile though this is, Carter makes it worse by blackmail. When Gabriel objects that he and his team are not contract killers, Carter says:

I could remind you that this president [Bush] has remained steadfastly at your side while the rest of the world has treated you as the Jew among nations. I could remind you that he allowed you to build the Separation Fence while the rest of the world accuses you of behaving like South Africans (p. 137).

The proposal is that Gabriel should put an agent into the "House of Zizi" and await the appearance there of Bin Shafiq. Gabriel agrees, and the agent will be Sarah after she has masqueraded as the art historian partner of Isherwood and indeed the person who had tracked down the missing Van Gogh. This whole conversation is so damning of American foreign policy that the criticism overrides its outdatedness. It may be even more relevant in 2016 (the date of this writing) than in 2006. As Gabriel says (after having agreed to take on the miserable chore), "Patience and follow-through aren't typical American virtues. You like to make a mess and move on to the next problem" (p. 142).

In fact, President Bush was recordedly weak or evasive on the Separation Fence (which its opponents called a Wall). After a meeting with Palestinian Prime Minister Abbas on July 25, 2003, in which he allowed Abbas's assertion that "the wall must come down," four days later, in a meeting with Ariel Sharon, he had changed the name of the problem from "wall" to "fence." In response to an Israeli journalist who demanded that he clarify his position and perhaps his terminology (an extraordinarily big issue), Bush replied wetly:

> *Look, the fence is a sensitive issue, I understand. And the Prime Minister (Abbas) made it very clear to me that it was a sensitive issue. And my promise to him is we'll continue to discuss and dialogue how best to make sure that the fence sends the right signal that not only is security important, but the ability for the Palestinians to live a normal life is important, as well.*

So here is a link to the major topic of the Holocaust series.

I hope I have given enough (but not too much) indication, not only of what the plot will consist but also of the higher ideological stakes in this novel. Now it is time to turn to one that seems at first out of the loop in that it mainly takes place in an entirely different environment, that is, England or Great Britain. It does, however, start in Amsterdam, where a Jewish scholar, Solomon Rosner, was murdered by a nondescript house painter devotee of Al-Qaeda. This is a direct result of the Islamization of the Netherlands that has been foolhardy in its acceptance of throngs of immigrants from the Middle East. And Silva has a strong interest in Egypt, which at this time was still under the rule of Hosni Mubarak and therefore another breeding ground Islamic terrorism.

THE SECRET SERVANT

But if "Amsterdam was well on its way to becoming a Muslim city" (p. 25), this was even more true of Britain, whose capital city had earned itself the sinister nickname of Londonistan. Having been sent first to Amsterdam to clean out Rosner's files and receiving there troubling information about an Al-Qaeda cell who are apparently on their way to London to wreak havoc, Gabriel too flies to London. There, he and the head of M15, Graham Seymour, discuss the ethnic crisis in Britain. An ethnic crisis simplifies the ethics of intervention even though a single intervention is like raising an umbrella in a field of tornadoes. Here, at some length, is Gabriel's view of the situation and its causes:

> *For two decades, beginning in the 1980s and continuing even after the attacks of 9/11, British governments both Labour and Tory had thrown open their doors to the world's most hardened holy warriors. Cast out by countries such as Egypt, Saudi Arabia, Jordan, and Syria, they had come to London, where they were free to publish, preach, organize, conspire, and raise money. As a result, Great Britain, the land of John Locke . . . had unwittingly allowed itself to become the primary incubator of a violent ideology that sought to destroy everything for which it once stood . . . [yet] responded by choosing the path of accommodation rather than resistance . . . The failure of this policy of appeasement had been held up for all the world to see on July 7, 2005, when three bombs exploded inside the London Underground and a fourth tore a London city bus to shreds in Tavistock Square. And all evidence*

suggested it was only their opening salvo. Her Majesty's security
services estimated the number of terrorists residing Britain as
sixteen thousand (pp. 63–64).

Gabriel has come to London to warn British security that something of equal magnitude is about to happen soon. Graham Seymour is unimpressed. He scorns the small amount of evidence Gabriel can produce and declines to raise the overall threat level. He will deeply regret it.

So where are we in time? *The Secret Servant* was copyrighted in 2007, two years after that "opening salvo." The British prime minister, who has rather a minimal role to play in this novel, was either Tony Blair or Gordon Brown, depending on which month we are in. The American president is still George W. Bush. His ambassador, however, is certainly not the elegant and generous Robert Halton conjured up by Silva but a man named Robert Tuttle, famous for his refusal to have the embassy pay the London traffic congestion charge. In 2007, the embassy owed 1.5 million pounds. Another form of terrorism? The U.S. ambassador needs to be elegant and likeable because the center of the plot is the abduction of his daughter on her run in Hyde Park, and the rest of the plot consists of Gabriel's attempts to get her back. Not only is she the ambassador's daughter, but she also is the president's goddaughter. This part of the plot takes entirely too long, and the elementary form of suspense generated by a series of false trails becomes rather irritating. We would be better off watching *Taken*. Of course, I will not reveal how Gabriel manages it; but, as usual, he is terribly damaged in the process.

Not so badly that he cannot go back to restoration, this time on a "Rembrandt panel, appropriately called St. Peter in prison" (p. 455). This Rembrandt exists and was given to the Israel Museum in Jerusalem by Judy and Michael Steinhard in 2005. A superbly naturalistic portrait, it shows the aged saint kneeling in a dark cell, his face and his hands and his famous keys beautifully illuminated. Obviously, there is an ironic relationship between the saint's imprisonment and the keys; but perhaps even more to the point, of the many painterly realizations of this biblical episode, this is the only one that does *not* record the angelic rescue. The light may indicate that it is on its way. But Silva's word "appropriately" demands that we ask the relevance of the painting's subject to the novel we are reading.

If the plot is too conventional, I was saddened to recognize that it replicates, not exactly but still distressingly, that of Lee Child's second Jack Reacher novel *Die Trying* (1998), where the goddaughter of the American

Rembrandt van Rijn, *Saint Peter in Prison* (1631). The Israel Museum, Jerusalem, Israel / Gift of Judy and Michael Steinhardt I Bridgeman Images.

president is also kidnapped, not by Islamic terrorists but by right-wing crazies who want to set up their own independent state in an unreachable area in Montana. Silva makes more serious use of this old, old plot device—the kidnapped maiden—but the analogy to *Die Trying* makes the device seem even more old-fashioned, particularly since it does not seem clear what exactly the terrorists hope to gain from this cruel exercise. To be sure, they want the release of a dying Sheikh, but he probably wouldn't last one year back in Egypt. Moreover, in its focus on "la fille mal gardée," who is, in fact, rather robust for an endangered maiden, the novel passes briskly over the *other* part of the terrorist mission: "Bombs had exploded in the Underground at Marble Arch, Piccadilly Circus, Leicester Square, and Charing Cross" (p. 101). "Three thousand dead, with more than two thousand injured" (p. 103), reports Graham Seymour, who had not thought it was worth raising the threat level. After the event, he sounds inured to yet another terrorist success—as perhaps we are all becoming.

That said, and said critically, the novel does raise serious geopolitical issues. Silva here extends his geographical range to Egypt, which is as much part of the problem as Saudi Arabia, also "churning out terrorists" (p. 290). The situation in Egypt when the novel was written is accurately described by Gabriel in part 3, interestingly titled "The Sacrifice of Isaac":

> *In many respects Egypt is already an Islamic republic. The Egyptian government is unable to provide the most basic services to its people and the Islamists have filled the void. They've penetrated the elementary schools and the universities, the bureaucracy and the trade unions, the arts and the press, even the courts and the legal guilds. No books can be published, and no film can be produced, that doesn't first meet the approval of the clerics . . . Western influences are slowly being extinguished. It's only a matter of time before the regime is extinguished too* (p. 291).

Well, as we know, the regime was extinguished in 2011 when a revolution overthrew Hosni Mubarak and installed a republic. But as of 2007, where our novel belongs, it is pertinent for Graham Seymour to say:

> *Wouldn't be wonderful if we could snap our fingers and create a vibrant and viable democracy along the banks of the Nile. But*

> *that's not going to happen any time soon, especially given our*
> *track record in Iraq. Which means we're stuck with Mubarak*
> *and his thuggish regime for the foreseeable future. He's a son of*
> *a bitch, but he's our son of a bitch* (p. 290).

This famous quotation, which has traveled anecdotally from Roosevelt on Somosa, the Nicaraguan dictator, to other presidents and other dictators, is not so much worn out as a self-accusatory cliché, summoning up years of corrupt American foreign policy. Yet to our surprise, in our privileged afterview, what Seymour thinks as long in the future a "viable democracy along the banks of the Nile" has, for the moment, been established in Egypt. For the moment, the Muslim Brothers seem in a subordinate position.

But from Silva's perspective in 2007, the Mubarak regime was beginning its death struggle, resulting in the incarceration and torture of any of its citizens deemed a danger. One of these was Gabriel's Egyptian informant, Ibrahim Fawaz, who had first warned him of the danger of a big new attack in Britain but had held back certain crucial facts. We are treated to an agonizing retrospective account of Ibrahim's torture by Mubarak's secret policemen, as also of his daughter, which was far, far worse. This invites an ethical discussion of the acceptability and efficacy, if any, of torture, which reappears in several spots in this novel (pp. 214–215) and others. But Ibrahim's dreadful tale emerges as a result of his beatings by Gabriel's henchmen. Is beating torture? Something feels badly wrong here. And why does the operation to monitor the phone of Ishak in Copenhagen need to be given the code name Moriah, "the hill in Jerusalem where God orders Abraham to sacrifice his only son" (p. 297)? We all know that the sacrifice is voided by an angel (unnamed) who provides a sheep in Isaac's place; and Abraham, having passed the greatest possible test of obedience, earned his role as the father of the Abrahamic religions; but Abraham/Ibrahim and Isaac/Ishak? The analogy is unavoidable, but in this story, both father and son will be killed, the father by the only son. Silva seems to be rewriting or unwriting Genesis, in the darkest possible mode.

On this note, we might do well to move on, not to the next novel published but to one that comes four books and four years later. *Portrait of a Spy* returns to the theme of dangerous Saudi influence in the world and in the American government. It also returns to the woman who, at the end of *The Messenger*, was holding her dying father in her arms and screaming for revenge.

Portrait Of A Spy

The woman who lay screaming on the street in Cannes, remember, was Nadia al-Bakari, the spoiled only daughter of Zizi al-Bakari, funder of terrorism, lover of art. She has to be brought back into the story because the Americans and the Israelis need her extraordinary wealth to set up, not a honey trap, but a money trap. They are trying to find the mastermind behind a new terrorist organization that seems to be replacing Al-Qaeda and, as the novel opens, executes three massive attacks in Paris, Copenhagen, and London's Covent Garden.

The novel was copyrighted in 2011, and its events seem to unspool in that very year as, for example, "in Egypt, Pharaoh had finally fallen" (p. 113), a reference to the ousting of Mubarak, a process that began in February 2011. The actual death of Osama bin Laden on May 2, 2011, is alluded to by Nadia as an event that had changed the terrorist map (p. 208). Yet there seems to be another time scheme, whereby Gabriel was working on the Rembrandt *Portrait of a Young Woman* in mid-January in Cornwall, disappearing to intervene in the Iranian threat (the subject of *The Rembrandt Affair*), returning to Cornwall for a "glorious summer" (p. 7), disappearing again on Remembrance Day (November 11) for a few days in London, where the above-mentioned terrorist attacks ruin his plans. It seems as if we must back up to 2010 to situate Gabriel in real time. The few days in London began with a visit to the gallery of Julian Isherwood, where Gabriel and Chiara were shown a mysterious dirty painting that Isherwood had discovered "in a great limestone pile along the Norfolk coast, current attribution of workshop of Palma Vecchio" that Isherwood had just acquired for twenty thousand pounds.

Both Gabriel and Chiara identified the painting, a *Virgin and Child with Mary Magdalen*, as a Titian, which means that Isherwood had pulled off a huge coup; and Gabriel agrees to restore it for two hundred thousand pounds, starting right away. This plan is violently interrupted by the terrorist attack on Covent Garden, where Gabriel and Chiara had gone to have a pleasant autumn lunch. But this painting "really" exists though it is safely located in the Hermitage in St. Petersburg. Its gentle emotions and quiet calm are remarkably therapeutic in the light of what happens next.

Unfortunately, Gabriel's presence at the terrorist attack in Covent Garden leads, first, to his arrest for being about to shoot the *shaheed* before he detonated his deadly vest and then his being drawn back into the world of antiterrorism by our old friend Adrian Carter of the CIA. Before their meeting, Silva treats us to a professional biography of Carter, which constitutes a mini-political history of most of the world since the Cold War, when he had served in British intelligence in Russia. When the Soviet Union collapsed, "the CIA had lost its very reason for existence" (p. 78). That had changed decisively with the attack on the Twin Towers, a victory personally claimed by Osama bin Laden, and it was the CIA that took over the job of tracking down his foot soldiers in Afghanistan:

> It was Carter, from his desk at Langley, who often served as their judge and jury. The black sites, the extraordinary renditions, the enhanced interrogation methods—they all bore Carter's fingerprints. He felt no remorse over his actions. He hadn't that luxury (p. 78).

Osama bin Laden will die in the course of this novel, historically on April 2, 2011, and his replacement will not be Isis but a mysterious man called Malik, whose current location it will be Gabriel's responsibility to discover. Unfortunately for our sense of ethics, these revelations about Carter's activities under the auspices of George W. Bush make us like him a lot less. And now there is a new president, obviously Obama, who, according to Carter, "views the global war on terrorism as a distraction from his larger goals" (p. 81). In other words, Carter is working on his own initiative, and the operation will have to be kept secret from the president, not an optimum mandate.

Titian, *Madonna and Child with Mary Magdalene* (1560). State
Hermitage Museum. Image is used from www.hermitagemusum.org,
courtesy of The State Hermitage Museum, St. Petersburg, Russia.

What makes Carter even more unattractive (and he will get worse) is that the current crisis is partly his fault. He had recruited a young Yemeni cleric named Rashid al-Husseini, who was possessed of "a beautiful and seductive tongue" (p. 85) and who presented himself as an Islamic moderate shocked and disgusted by 9/11. Carter sent him out into the Middle East to spread the doctrine of moderation on CIA money. Hey presto, within three years of making contacts and building cells on Carter's "dime," the "enlightened young man of moderation was gone. He'd been replaced by a raving fanatic who preached that the only way to deal with the West was to destroy it" (p. 89). Naturally, this was not something that Carter wanted widely known. Hence, the extreme secrecy under which Gabriel was being asked to operate. Obama was to know nothing, and especially to be kept in the dark was his incompetent but meddling assistant to the president on Homeland Security, James McKenna. In return, Gabriel was to receive all the sensitive information on Rashid and his case and on the three attacks. To sweeten the deal, if deal it were, Carter provides Gabriel with an assistant of his own, one whom we are glad to welcome back, the fetching and courageous Sarah Bancroft, who is now a CIA agent.

The search for Rashid by Gabriel's team, specifically Dina, turns up another more dangerous name, Malik al-Zubair. Sprouted in the Zarqua refugee camp in Jordan, half Palestinian and half Syrian, he cut his teeth working for Hamas and then moved on to Iraq, where he executed several major bombings against Shiites and then "decided it was time to go international" (p. 125). A shape-shifter, he had proved impossible to track and will eventually use one of the most effective disguises to ruin the Nadia plan created by Gabriel, who is disastrously outwitted.

I must say *something* about the Nadia plan, for it is very complicated. It is she who becomes one of the most effective spies the CIA has ever deployed but only after the recruitment of the most sophisticated and, for the reader, entertaining kind. Her recruitment involves yet another woman, the famous British reporter Zoe Reed, who, of course, had herself to be recruited in the intervening novel *The Rembrandt Affair*. Once drawn in, Nadia can draw on her own deep regrets for her father's career, which outweigh her sorrow at his death and undertake adventures unspeakably dangerous to herself. The first stage is the "money trap," which involves the Titian, which Nadia will "purchase" for the astonishing sum of fifty million pounds in a throat-clenching auction of Viennese art at Christie's in the first week in February 2011. This is not at all like the Van Gogh used to lure her father. It is a heavily sanctioned money laundering. Theoretically, the painting had been "owned" by Oliver Dimbleby, who was in on the scheme for a ludicrously small amount by Samir Abbas, a middle man with many jihadist credentials. It was then put up for auction, though nobody knew who the mysterious second buyer was. When the big money came in, Abbas redirected it around the world to so many terrorist cells that Gabriel and his team can hardly believe how well the scheme has worked. Where the money goes, it reveals its presence to the antiterrorism authorities. It is in the enthusiasm created by this success that Nadia is asked to do more of the same, face-to-face with the dangerous Malik.

This plot device allows Silva to return to the problem of Saudi Arabia in more detail and with more force. The problem derives from Wahhabi doctrine, the severest version of Islam in the region, and the devil's compact between Wahhabism and the Saudi monarchy, which dates back to 1744 when an "austere reformist preacher named Muhammad Abdul" formed an alliance with a Nejdi tribe called the Al-Saud, "thus creating the union of political and religious power that would eventually lead to the . . . modern state of Saudi Arabia, (p. 294). In a dialogue between Gabriel and his mentor Shamron, it is explained to us that now, ten years after 9/11, after which "the Saudis promised to put an end to the incitement that gave rise to Bin Laden and al-Quaeda," things have gone back to normal, as it were. Saudi money, says Shamron, "is once again fueling the hatred, with scarcely a word of protest from the Americans" (p. 188). To make matters more complicated, asserts Shamron, the Americans are receiving a great deal of information, most of it useless, from Saudi intelligence about potential plots. The Saudis are playing both sides of the street and have so far been successful in currying favor with the current American President, Barak Obama. But when informed of Nadia's role in the upcoming operation, he lays down his passivity and lurches in the opposite direction, insisting that the White House and Langley have control over it, leaving the Israelis, who have set it up, to pack up their tents and go home. It takes considerable negotiation to reverse this idiotic though perhaps chivalric decree. Finally, it is agreed that Gabriel's team "would be allowed to retain their ascendancy in the field so long as the operation did not touch the sacred soil of Saudi Arabia . . . The president would not permit Israeli intelligence to make mischief in the land of Mecca and Medina"(p. 262).

But the President hadn't counted on disobedience from Nadia herself. Without informing anyone, including her own bodyguard, she directs her driver to take her into the Nejd desert for a personal interview with Sheikh Marwan bin Tayib, dean of the department of theology at the University of Mecca. So we are exposed to the views of a hostile Islamic man who insults her at every turn. She needs him, however, to act as liaison with Rashid and behind him Malik. And we need her to see through her eyes and hear through her ears the primitive state in which the Saudis live when not in their gilded palaces and the parlous condition of their women, who exist (almost completely) segregated from men, with only one another for company, without education of any kind; they are merely breeding animals, and heaven forfend that their products should be female.

Nadia's ploy was successful. She received a telephone call, inviting her to a meeting with Malik in a seven-star hotel in Dubai, an enclave that Gabriel's team, though with many doubts, concluded was civilized enough for the meeting to go forward. Compared to Saudi Arabia, Dubai is a reasonably tolerant country, relying mostly on tourism and shopping for its income, both of which would be damaged by high-level scandal. Nadia herself is unafraid or rather undeterred. But she too is outsmarted by Malik, about whom Dina had remarked, "Heaven help us all." It did not. I will not tell you how, nor the secret reason why she allowed herself to be used in this manner, because Nadia's role was ultimately to influence the art world far more than the political one.

Gabriel returns to Cornwall to recuperate from the whole Saudi disaster. Sarah sends him a commission, to paint a full-length, gorgeous, bejeweled portrait of Nadia to be hung in MOMA. "It was a portrait of an unveiled woman. A portrait of a martyr. It was a portrait of a spy" (p. 482). It is now midsummer 2011. As usual, the work heals him. But it is not restoration in the usual sense. He has to create the image out of his imagination, and you can do so too. There are no prototypes among the Old Masters or the Impressionists, the two sources to which the novel itself directs us (p. 481). "He hung pearls around her neck and adorned her hands with diamonds and gold. A clock face shone moonlike over her shoulder. Orchids lay at her bare feet. For several days, he struggled with the background. In the end he chose to depict her rising out of Caravaggesque darkness" (p. 481). And he refused to sign the painting, thereby creating a small local mystery. The Nadia al-Bakari Wing of MOMA was formally opened on the anniversary of 9/11, and Sarah's speech at the event was "part eulogy, part call to action" against the forces of destruction unleashed that day. Perhaps more to the point, given Silva's own program for making novels themselves a call to action, Sarah managed in her speech "to walk the fine line between truth and fiction" (p. 488).

Meanwhile, in the United States, the successful rolling up of dozens of enemy cells was completed; and the president (Obama) was said to have just "guaranteed himself another four years in office. The race for 2012 was over. It was time to start thinking about 2016" (p. 334). This is wildly premature. Malik is still out there, so is Rashid, but not for long.

Since I have created, as Silva did not from the start intend to do, a Saudi sequence that disrupts the chronology created by mere publication dates, the reader might reasonably ask why. To me, it seems evident that Silva came to see the problem of Saudi Arabia in the world as more sinister than he had at first thought. But possibly, his gloom was premature or insufficiently mobile. In 2007, the year in which Silva published *The Messenger*, the popular American view of the Saudis was dire. In that year, John R. MacArthur complained about "the vast power of the Saudi Lobby," which depends on the supply to the United States of oil at supportable rates for consumers; "In exchange we arm the Saudis to the teeth and turn a blind eye to their medieval approach to crime and punishment," hence our failure to defend the democracy protesters in Bahrain. This was *part* of the real state of affairs to which Gabriel and Adrian Carter referred in *The Messenger*, Gabriel in frustration, Carter in nonchalant resignation (p. 139). "This is not the time to tear down the House of Saud" (p. 139), said Carter. But by 2011, when *Portrait of a Spy* was published, this opinion was shaky at best and on the verge of being obsolete. King Abdullah was, had been, a reformer. His achievements included judicial reforms, especially reeducating Sharia's judges; educational opportunities for women, including the coed King Abdullah University for Science and Technology; and encouraging religious toleration by promoting interfaith dialogue, culminating in an important conference in Spain in July 2008. He advised against the Bush invasion of Iraq but quietly helped out anyway. And in the light of the Arab Spring, seeing its warnings for himself, in 2011, he poured thirty-seven billion dollars of his own money into the country to be used in jobless benefits, education, housing subsidies, and *a new sports channel*. Call it bribery. Call it reform. Call it savvy.

The concept of spoiler chains me. Carefully avoiding giving away any more of the plot than I have, suffice it to say that the search for Rashid turns up another, more dangerous name, a seasoned international terrorist whom it falls to Nadia al-Bakari to identify and locate. This involves recruitment at its highest, most sophisticated, and most tragic level since Nadia herself must first be hunted and then persuaded to right some of the wrongs that her very bad father, Zizi, had committed or enabled. In this endeavor, the Titian plays more than a subsidiary role, more than esthetic salve. It becomes a tool. It becomes something that Nadia will purchase for the astonishing sum of fifty million pounds in a throat-clenching auction of Viennese art at Christie's in the first week in February. We have turned the corner from late 2010 to 2011 evidently.

We are also evidently involved in heavily sanctioned money laundering. The painting had earlier been "bought" from Oliver Dimbleby, who was in on the scheme for a ludicrously small amount by Samir Abbas, a middle man with many jihadist credentials. When the big money came in, Abbas redirected it around the world to so many terrorist cells that Gabriel and his team can hardly believe how well the scheme has worked. Where the money goes, it reveals its presence to the antiterrorism authorities. It is in the enthusiasm created by this success that Nadia is asked to do more of the same, face-to-face as it were, with the master terrorists in Saudi Arabia; and this extension goes severely wrong, resulting in her murder. But as her monument, Museum of Modern Art in New York (MOMA) opens a special wing to house and display her astonishing collection of modern art. As for the Titian, it was returned to Julian Isherwood, its discoverer, and donated by him, despite its "real" presence in the Hermitage, to the National Gallery in London. If you want to think of this as a tiny art historical coup against Russia, you may.

INTERNATIONAL
ART THEFT

Art Theft And
International Politics

Silva's faithful readers, if they are reading his novels as they appear, will soon discover that the next three form retrospectively another series, this time focusing on the role of famous art as something more than itself. Instead of being Gabriel's leisure occupation, what he does when he is not fighting violence, his brilliant restoration of old masters has been expanded into an analysis of the role of famous paintings in the modern world. In this analysis, the theft of great paintings takes a central role. That these thefts have become endemic tells us a great deal about the parlous state of the societies in which we live, their failure to protect their masterpieces in museums and galleries a comment on how they got their priorities wrong; or did they? How much would it cost to protect them absolutely? And why? Why are they hung in public galleries in the first place, usually a long way away from where they were created, and for whom? But would we prefer them to disappear into the security of rich men's houses, where almost nobody could see them? And how is it they have acquired so great a monetary value that they can be substituted for cash by the Mafia or become reserves of private wealth as hedge funds, as it were, against the fall of tyrants; or as money laundering; or as currency. Silva has already touched on this subject in *Portrait of a Spy*, where the device to send a river of money flowing into terrorist cells was engineered by a very high-priced auction for a newly discovered Titian purchased by Nadia al-Bakari.

These three novels move gradually toward the concept of a *Heist*, the title of the third in the series. We think of heists usually with a certain amount of tolerance, as in train robbers or the genial hijinks of caper movies. In November 2011, a movie titled *The Tower Heist* will offered up a new cast of genial villains, whose success we are meant to applaud. However, in real life, there really occurred the thefts detailed in the *Rembrandt Affair* (pp. 10–11). The recoveries announced in *The Heist* (p. 464), however, are fictional. Facts are much less gratifying. And Silva's *Heist* actually reinvents the term and turns it back toward purely (or impurely) monetary skulduggery. That this is carried out by Gabriel is disturbing, as we shall see.

The Rembrandt Affair

This is the first Gabriel Allon novel to focus on, as distinct from mentioning, Gabriel's second (or is it his first) career, not assassination but art restoration. The title makes it clear that the novel's heart is a great painting by Rembrandt, which caused many things to happen in Gabriel's world. In this case, the painting does not come into Gabriel's hands for restoration until the very end of the novel; it has been stolen, and his assignment from the forever lovable Julian Isherwood is to find it. The painting has to work hard, however, to keep together the seemingly quite separate strands of narrative. Silva is conjuring. This novel makes connections to two of his earlier themes, the Holocaust and the up-to-date problem of the Middle East; in this case, the main plot or theme is art theft, which is said to be out of control all over the world where art museums and galleries exist.

But this is linked to the story of Lena Herzfeld and how she survived the Holocaust when her parents and sister were both shipped off to a concentration camp; survived because she had blond hair and because her father "sold" the Rembrandt in question to Kurt Voss of the SS in exchange for her life. This echoes the hard past of Julian Isherwood, carried as a child out of occupied France in 1942 by a pair of Basque shepherds, while his father, the renowned Paris art dealer, Samuel Isakowitz, was sent to the death camp at Sobibor, a tale appropriately retold here (p. 30). And both connect to the tale of Hannah Weinberg in *The Messenger*, who owns a fabled Van Gogh painting because her father in 1942 hid it from the Nazis under the floorboards. Likewise, the Voss plot reintroduces the Ratline theme, of the help given to fleeing Nazis by the Vatican, and the nauseating behavior of the Swiss banking industry.

Silva's concern with the threats from the Middle East resurfaces here in what seems like a quite different story, the effort to sabotage the attempts of Iran to construct nuclear arms. This plot introduces a villain analogous to Kurt Voss, another German who himself profited exorbitantly from the Holocaust. Kurt Voss had placed his stolen assets, including this Rembrandt, in a small Swiss bank run by Walter Landesmann; and when he sent his wife after the war to collect them, the bank denied knowing anything about it. Thus, the assets were twice stolen; and the eventual recipient of this fortune was Landesmann's son, now famous for munificent giving to the world's neediest and most deserving causes. St. Martin, he had come to be called. Is this reparation? By no means. This thread introduces the famous British reporter Zoe Reed, whom my readers (thanks to my messing with the chronology of publication) have already met. She had been the agent of Gabriel's recruitment of Nadia al-Bakari in *Portrait of a Spy*, which actually followed *The Rembrandt Affair* by a couple of years. Here, she is actually sent into the villain's house, along with Mikhail, to infiltrate his computers. She is very nearly killed, another instance of Gabriel's willingness to send his women into danger. Thanks to Zoe's courage here, in a task much scarier than the recruitment of Nadia, Gabriel and his team are able to learn that Saint Martin, behind his masque of sanctity and numerous international intermediaries, has been supplying the Islamic Republic of Iran with the centrifuges that they need to move their nuclear program forward. This knowledge will permit the act of international sabotage whereby (and we are not told precisely how) the American, Israeli, and British security heads manage to take out the centrifuges in the four underground facilities in Iran. The Iranians are caught in a mighty deception. At the end of *The Rembrandt Affair*, this part of the plot concludes with one word: Boom (p. 507).

We now know, of course, that this novel, which appeared in 2010, lost much of its warning force when Iran agreed, after several years of crippling economic sanctions, to cease production of nuclear weapons. This was largely thanks to the leadership of the new American President, Barak Obama, who is still vilified by some Republicans for what they see as American weak knees, and his able Secretary of State, John Kerry. A year from now, this development too may be outdated. But in 2014, a deal was made, over the fierce opposition of Israel, to reduce the international sanctions against Iran in exchange for limitations on its nuclear program. The deal lowered Iran's program of enrichment from nineteen thousand centrifuges to six thousand, and inspectors were allowed to monitor the supply chain. Once again, Silva was ahead of the curve.

But the real plot here is the Rembrandt, which involves another damaged woman. Her provenance is more than usually complex, not least because we are dealing with fiction. "She had been sold in Amsterdam in 1936 to a man named Abraham Herzfeld, acquired by coercion in 1943 by an S.S. officer named Kurt Voss, and sold twenty-one years later in a private transaction conducted by the Hoffmann Gallery of Lucerne" (pp. 496–497). This is all that was told to the public when she came up for auction in London. In between, she had been hidden in Martin Landesmann's small Swiss bank and, early in 2010, was offered for sale by, presumably, Martin Landesmann. Here, even the "official" provenance can drive you crazy with what it does not explain or perhaps what it forgets. The sale was arranged by David Cavendish, "art advisor to the vastly rich, and a rather shady character" (p. 35), and Julian Isherwood, who negotiated with the National Gallery a price of forty-five million. The painting was then sent to a restorer, Christopher Liddell, because Gabriel was deemed not sufficiently restored himself after his ordeal in Saudi Arabia. Liddell was murdered and the painting stolen. In the course of this violent theft, the painting acquired a coat of blood and a bullet hole. The theft had been arranged by a crooked middleman, Maurice Durand, (whom we have met before) into whose hands in Paris the canvas was conveyed by his thief, Yves Morel. Having discovered the painting's guilty secret, a list of Jewish names and hence bank accounts hidden behind the canvas, Durand immediately concluded that the painting was too hot to hold and took it, in its cardboard tube, to his friend Angelique Brossard for very safe keeping. But he also, apparently, kept and entrusted the incriminating list of Jewish names to Hannah Weinberg, who was persuaded to hand them over to Eli Lavon, a member of the Israeli team. Finally, we are told, inexplicably, that the painting "had been quietly left in an alley behind a synagogue . . . in the Marais section of Paris" (p. 491) and therefrom conveyed to Isherwood, who would pass it to Gabriel in Cornwall for restoration. After three months, it would be displayed at the National Gallery of Art's "long awaited Rembrandt, A Retrospective" (p. 491). In the intermission, it had been returned to Lena Hirschfeld, the rightful owner, who gifted it to the museum that had previously agreed to buy it for forty-five million dollars.

If this does not make you dizzy, consider the following problem. When Gabriel, now in possession of the damning list of Jewish accounts, confronts Martin Landesmann, he remarks, "You continued to look for a lost masterpiece by Rembrandt that had the power to destroy you" (p. 475). Yet someone offered to sell the painting at the beginning of the story, and who could that have been but Saint Martin? The seller is described by Cavendish as "some sort of humanitarian" (p. 36). Did Silva himself lose track of the trail? Could Martin have offered it for sale without realizing what it contained as "the most expensive envelope in history"? At any rate, this mistake, if it is one, pales beside the deal that Gabriel is offering Martin. It is, bleakly, blackmail. Rather than bringing him down (by exposing the list so that he can be "torn to shreds by the class-action lawyers in America") and having tracked his business relationships with Iran that can also be made public, Gabriel offers him, of all things, a partnership. What has happened to the ethics of this series? True, the partnership makes it possible to sabotage much of the Iranian nuclear program, at least for the time being. But Landesmann makes my point for me: "Do you see no ethical issue in the intelligence service of the State of Israel profiting from the sale of gas centrifuges to the Islamic Republic of Iran?" (p. 480) That the centrifuges will shortly be disabled does not take away the pain of the question.

It is high time to identify this particular Rembrandt as *Portrait of a Young Woman*, painted in the mid-1650s. Thus, the "she" to whom I have been referring is, was, a real woman. Disingenuous as usual, Silva assures us in his "Author's Note" to this novel that the portrait on which it is based "could never have been stolen, for it does not exist." However, "if there were such a painting, it would look markedly like *Portrait* of *Hendrickje Stoffels* . . . which hangs in Room 23 of the National Gallery in London" (p. 521). A detail of this portrait is tipped into the Signet edition. It is pretty much established, despite the usual sceptics, that this is a portrait of a young woman who entered Rembrandt's household about 1649, initially as housekeeper and nurse to his young son Titus and soon afterward became his mistress. This factual knowledge gives the portrait unusual depth, which then, though extraneous to it, in turn, deepens the novel.

There is a fine description of the effects and intentions of this portrait by Jonathan Jones in the *Guardian* for July 15, 2000:

> *There is the irresistible suggestion of the aftermath of sex in this painting . . . Hendrickje is wearing a fur wrap, a gold necklace, pearl earrings and jewels in her hair. Under the wrap she is wearing a white shift, but it doesn't hide much. She's relaxed about showing the painter her breasts, her naked throat. The fur and the jewels heighten rather than hide her nakedness . . . Hendrickje is located in a dark, private, interior space in which she and the artist share their deepest secrets. The redness that burns on the left of the painting is deliberately unfinished, heightening the impressionistic casualness. Rembrandt uses these painterly pleasures to make us feel the physical presence of Hendrickje; the milky texture of the fur makes us aware of our own flesh and therefore hers. Her body is substantial and adult; her hand is sculpted, monumental, her face not idealized but real. Hendrickje's eyes are big, black pools full of thought. It's the consciousness behind those eyes that makes you pause before this painting, convinced you are looking at someone who is looking back at you with complete intimacy.*

As an ekphrasis, always a difficult act to pull off, this seems exactly right. Jones goes on to remind us that in 1654, Hendrickje appeared before the Church Council of Amsterdam, accused of "living in whoredom with the painter Rembrandt." "This painting answers the charge of whoredom not by denying sex but glorifying it." But Rembrandt went on to paint Hendrickje in several other versions or stages of her life, including *Young Woman in Bed* in the National Gallery of Scotland, which is by no means adoring but rather sweatily voluptuous, a portrait of the same woman rather heavily clothed and evidently sad in the Metropolitan Museum in New York, and *Woman at an Open Door* in the Gemäldegalerie in Berlin. It has been suggested, perhaps as a way to avoid the biographical so-called fallacy, that Hendrickje's portrait was one of a series of portraits of courtesans, a theme that was popular in Holland at the time; and *Woman at an Open Door* has been plausibly said to be based on one of Palma Vecchio's examples of the genre. But in other versions, Hendrikje gets both older and sadder, no doubt responding to Rembrandt's refusal to marry her despite

Rembrandt van Rijn, *Portrait of Hendrickje Stoffels* (probably 1654-1656). National Gallery, London. © National Gallery, London / Art Resource, NY.

all the care she gave him as he aged. For those who believe, as I do, in biographical interpretation, Silva's title, *The Rembrandt Affair*, acquires a second meaning.

The first view that Gabriel and Chiara have of the painting is from ten photographs supplied by Isherwood, one entire canvas and nine close-up details. Typically, they have different responses. He speaks only about its being "two and a half centuries ahead of its time" (p. 51) in its anticipation of Impressionism, but it is Chiara from whom we get another brief ekphrasis: "Pretty girl. Rembrandt's mistress? . . . He treated her shabbily. He should have married her." And several pages later, "I think she looks pregnant. Do you know what else I think? She's keeping a secret. She knows she's pregnant but hasn't worked up the courage to tell him." This entirely different perspective (though, of course, Silva has created it also) gives the portrait even more human value. It is Chiara who determines that the search must begin: "I can't leave a pregnant woman buried in a hole, Gabriel, and neither can you" (pp. 56–57). This connects back to Chiara's brutal experience in *The Defector*, where she involuntarily aborted an eight-week fetus "in a hole" of a Russian prison. She was in Russia because she had hidden the fact of her pregnancy from Gabriel.

Expanding on the portrait itself in this way and the real story that lies behind it allows one to have a better feeling about the novel as a whole as it draws to a close. Silva cleverly capitalizes on our natural wish for better feelings by vivifying Hendrikje once more:

> By the time Gabriel and Chiara arrived in America, [after the restoration] their silent but demanding houseguest of three months was an international sensation. Her celebrity was not instant; it was rooted in an affair she'd had four hundred years earlier with a painter named Rembrandt and by the long and tragic road she had traveled ever since. Once upon a time, she would have been forced to live out her days in shame. Now they were lining up for tickets just to have a glimpse of her (p. 496).

And in the National Gallery of Art in Washington, she is safe at last. However, in real life as distinct from *The Rembrandt Affair*, she was purchased in 1976 from the Walter Morrison Pictures Settlement by private treaty for an undisclosed sum and not shown to the public until 1978 because of her need for major cleaning. The publicity surrounding the acquisition provides a much less colorful provenance, she having been quietly in the possession of Walter Morrison and his family since 1838.

THE FALLEN ANGEL

The Fallen Angel is, of course, a phrase obsessed with its past, in the history of Christianity, and particularly, in John Milton's *Paradise Lost*, which explores with unsurpassable sophistication the theological paradox that an angel, created perfect, could fall. We have to start with the question as to whether our own angel, Gabriel Allon, is fallen, and if so, why. This should make us revisit the whole ethical crux of Gabriel's operations on behalf of Israel, of the revenge ethos, and of the dubiously asserted necessity of securing one's own territory at any cost. Because that, of course, is what Israel is—territory—carved by fiat out of the territory of others. Toward the end of the novel, we are reminded that the great instigator of violence on the Israeli side has been Ari Shamron, who, despite the hitch in Iran's nuclear program that Gabriel arranged in *The Rembrandt Affair*, is still contemplating what must be a nuclear attack on Iranian nuclear facilities (p. 320). Otherwise, "the beautiful country that [he] helped to create and defend collapses" (p. 320). If Gabriel is a fallen angel, Shamron, the *memuneh*, is worse.

The novel starts with a great fall, not of an angel but of a woman, Claudia Andreotti, who had been employed by the Vatican to conduct an inventory of its art holdings, perhaps an overdue routine, perhaps on the suspicion that some of them might be missing. Claudia is found dead on the tiled floor of the Basilica of St. Peter's, having evidently fallen from a great height—the viewing platform of the great dome. The papal secretary Donati, whom we have met several times before, immediately decides to call upon Gabriel as he has more than once previously; but this time Donati internally describes him as "a fallen angel in black. A sinner in the city of saints" (p. 7).

Caravaggio, *The Deposition* (1600-1604). Pinacoteca, Vatican
Museums. Photo courtesy Scala / Art Resource, NY.

Red figure Calyx-Krater depicting the body of Sarpedon lifted by Hypnos and Thanatos in the presence of Hermes, Leodamas, and Hippolytos (c. 515 BCE). Signed by Euphronios (painter) and Euxitheosas (potter). Museo Nazionale di Villa Giulia, Rome. Photo courtesy Scala / Ministero per i Beni e le Attività culturali / Art Resource, NY.

Perhaps appropriately, Gabriel has been roused from his current piece of restoration, that of "Caravaggio's *Deposition of Christ*, widely regarded as Caravaggio's finest painting" (p. 12). Painted in 1603, this was clearly an adaptation of Raphael's version of the scene (1507); and its extremely diagonal design has been copied by artists as diverse as Rubens, Fragonard, Gericault, and Cezanne. Like all of Caravaggio's paintings, this says Realism, Naturalism, especially in the well-muscled legs of Nicodemus, who lowers the dead body to a slab of stone and indeed in the torso of Christ himself. This is not the first Caravaggio that Gabriel has restored. In *The Defector*, he had been working on *The Crucifixion of St. Peter*, a peculiarly ugly representation that uses the diagonal format in reverse and makes the saint's face insignificant compared to the buttocks and bent legs of one of his torturers. This was Realism in your face. One might even see the "Deposition" as an aesthetic apology for the *Crucifixion*. I dwell on this because the last great painting to engage Gabriel is another Caravaggio, the stolen *Nativity with St. Francis and St. Lawrence*, to discover which will be his ultimate goal in *The Heist*. Caravaggio himself, of course, was rather a fallen angel.

But unlike the Rembrandt portrait of Hendrikje, the *The Deposition* has no agency of its own and does nothing to integrate the three main plots of *The Fallen Angel*. The first of these is a simple murder mystery. If Claudia Andreotti did not fall of her own volition, as Gabriel is quick to ascertain, then who killed her, and why? Asking this question leads Gabriel, with Chiara at his side, into the middle of another kind of art theft, the traffic in stolen antiquities, especially Attic vases. Shortly, he will find himself in front of the *Euphronios Krater*, "regarded as one of the greatest single pieces of art ever created," which had been looted and sold to the Metropolitan Museum of Art in New York. Now it has returned to something resembling its own geographical location, a glass-covered pedestal in the Villa Guilia, "Italy's national repository of Etruscan art and antiquities" (p. 12). This raises in Gabriel's mind and in mine a question comparable to one I raised earlier. Who should own art, and where is it best displayed?

> *Cultural patrimony had been protected, thought Gabriel, looking round the uninhabited room, but at what cost? Nearly five million people visited the Met each year, but here, in the*

deserted halls of the Villa Guilia, the krater was left to stand
alone with the sadness of a knickknack gathering dust on a
shelf (p. 90).

On the *Krater* is brilliantly portrayed "the lifeless body of Sarpedon, son of Zeus, being carried off for burial. The image was strikingly similar to the composition of *The Deposition of Christ*" (p. 91). In other words, the history of art has certain needs of its own that might sometimes override cultural nationalism.

Now the discovery of the *Krater* in the Metropolitan Museum of Art, the further discovery that it had no clean provenance, and its triumphant return to Italy are in no way fiction. This episode opens up a large of chunk of real art and political history to which Silva actually points by mentioning Giacomo Medici (pp. 81–83), an inveterate antiquities thief whose operation, says Wikipedia, "was thought to be one of the largest and most sophisticated antiquities network in the world, responsible for illegally digging up and spiriting a way thousands of top-drawer pieces and passing them on to the most elite end of the international art market." By this time, says General Ferrarro, the head of the Italian Art Squad in the novel, Medici is out of business. In fact, he was sentenced in 2004 by a Rome court to ten years in prison. But here, he seems to have been replaced by other figures whom Silva feels free to invent, middleman Roberto Falcone, found by Gabriel in a vat of acid and the top man, whose job it will be for Gabriel to smoke out. Silva will substitute this sinister figure for Robert Hecht, who was also very much a real figure, indicted in 2005 for conspiracy to traffic in illegal antiquities. A 1995 raid on a warehouse in Geneva found it stuffed with stolen ceramics and even statues. The case against Hecht failed because the statute of limitations wore out.

So it is not hard to see where Silva got his material. But something goes very wrong here with the book's ethics. Gabriel will be guilty of himself arranging for the theft from a rich man's house of a "lovely hydra by the Amykos painter" (p. 384), which he subsequently shatters and uses the fragments as a lure to find his way in to the trade in stolen antiquities. Fallen angelic technique, for sure, and some of it is Silva's, for in the last chapter, there is announced its "unexpected recovery" (p. 384) with no mention of its repair. Did the owner not notice the cracks?

Eventually, Gabriel learns that the mastermind behind the lucrative business in stolen antiquities is a hugely wealthy man, Carlo Marchese, who also has privileged access to the Vatican Bank, which he uses as a vehicle to ferry funds to, of all groups, Hesbollah. This is where Ari Shamron gets back into the driver's seat and instructs Gabriel to cut off this major source of funding to one of Israel's most troublesome enemies. How this is accomplished must remain a secret for now, but it has a certain poetic grandeur.

But before providing that poetic ending, *The Fallen Angel* swerves back into all-too-familiar territory, Arab terrorism, and Gabriel's role in countering it. This requires another daring act of kidnapping, reminiscent of the grabbing of the ex-Nazi Radek. In this case, the captive, Massoud, originally from Lebanon, has become an agent of Iranian intelligence, the dreaded Vevak. Under what Gabriel euphemistically calls "physical coercion," (cf. enhanced interrogation), Massoud will provide the necessary information to avert a terrorist attack on the Stadttempel synagogue in Vienna. So concludes the second major plot. Not very effectively in my view.

In the third plot, however, not only do we return to the theme of antiquities and the evidence of previous civilization left in the ground, but the stakes are much larger as well. The general thesis that this conflict will never end is supported by the fact that immediately after the Israeli office celebrated the success of this operation ("an old adversary had been severely compromised"), another problem arises. It involves our favorite pope, who has scheduled a visit to the Holy Land in Holy Week. Not ideal timing! Who could they get to dissuade him? "A fallen angel in black" (p. 284).

So at this point, without further ceremony, we are thrust into main plot 3, which consists of the pope's untimely visit to Israel (since Gabriel was entirely unable to persuade him otherwise) and a completely unconnected plot by Imam Hassan Darwish, one of the Wafq, the Arab caretakers of the Temple Mount. His plan is to bring down, in a tremendous explosion from underground, the Al-Aqsa Mosque, "the third holiest shrine in Islam" (p. 294), thereby precipitating the Third Intifada. This seems a clumsy and destructive way to create another Arab uprising against Israel. In the course of this plot, Darwish has uncovered but concealed archeological evidence of the existence of the First Temple of the Jews, something that the Arabs have always denied, twenty-two limestone pillars that had been part of the heikh of King Solomon's First Temple. Blowing the whole place up therefore had a double mission—one, to make Israel seemingly the destroyer of the Mount and two, to rewrite history in favor of the

Arabs. This plot is loosely connected to the second one by way of the idea of archeology as the key to past civilizations; and indeed, the twenty-two pillars, which correspond to biblical accounts of the First Temple, would soon, within the fiction of this novel, be transported to a purpose-built Israel museum. Clearly, one cannot argue that they will not have been restored to their proper place. The only problem is that this entire episode is unmitigated fiction.

But this is much too simply put. In this novel, the question of what is fact and what is fiction is raised in its most tendentious form by Silva himself, who connects it to the problem of Temple Denial, itself a fiction now cultivated by the Arabs. If there never were a Temple on the Mount, then there is no proof that the Jews had a prior claim to the territory. In his Author's Notes, Silva attributes this new myth to Yasir Arafat, who announced at the Camp David summit in 2000 that the Temple had stood not in Jerusalem but in Nablus" (p. 398). By "finding" archeological evidence of the Solomonic structure and mighty solid evidence at that (not merely shelves of artifacts), Silva makes the fiction of Temple Denial fictionally controverted. Brilliantly, he attributes to a German archeologist of the school of biblical minimalism the following dismissal: "twenty-two hunks of wishful thinking" (p. 378). But of course, the wishful thinking is Silva's (and Eli Lavon's, who almost died for it). And I have to admit that I now see the pillars in my mind though they are not on display in the new wing of the Israeli museum.

THE HEIST

As compared to *The Fallen Angel*, *The Heist*, the last novel in this series about stolen art, does not engage in wishful thinking, except in a few moments toward the end. General Ferrari, a character carried over from the earlier novel, announces the recovery of many famous lost paintings, some of which, like Klimt's *Portrait of a Woman* and Modigliani's *Woman with a Fan*, are, in fact, still missing and for which we still yearn (pp. 464–465).

But let me not quibble. *The Heist* offers up a clear single plot: Gabriel's quest, on behalf of General Ferrari, to recover what in the course of the novel comes to be seen by the reader as the world's most important missing painting: Caravaggio's *Nativity with St. Francis and St. Lawrence*, stolen from the Oratorio di San Lorenzo in 1969. This is very clever since it magnifies the nonmonetary worth of the painting exorbitantly and makes its recovery more pressing than seems called for in the troubled world that Gabriel inhabits. At the center of that troubled world, in this novel, is Syria, and the man in control, Assad, here referred to as the Butcher Boy, whose tyrannical rule is the most disastrous result of the ill-fated Arab Spring. The use of famous paintings in this novel is as a lure that Gabriel thinks might lead him to those who have put the Caravaggio "in play", as it is called when rumors that mention it begin to circulate.

The novel opens with a gruesome scene, first discovered by Julian Isherwood and then revisited by Gabriel in his detective mode: the mutilated body of a man called Jack Bradshaw, who, it seems, after a terrible downturn in his career, had become a dealer in stolen paintings. Jack had a vault in the Geneva Freeport full of stolen paintings, including, incidentally, *Woman with a Fan* by Modigliani, also an extraordinary letter addressed to Gabriel, but not the Caravaggio. The letter reveals that Bradshaw had had the painting, previously circulating as Mafia currency, for several months and had perhaps engaged to restore it. But he did not deliver, hence his murder. But where has he hidden it? That is for the reader to discover.

To smoke out the putative buyer, Gabriel has to put out an art famous bait, in this case, one of Van Gogh's paintings of *Sunflowers* hung not too safely in Amsterdam. Since he has already added to his credentials the title of art thief and enters again into collusion with Maurice Durand, this is pretty straightforward. All he has to do is to copy the painting, easy for him, and advertise its presence on the market.

If that were all that *The Heist* had to offer, nobody would be much interested. But this art plot is carefully entwined with another, to damage the ruler of Syria by getting inside his finances, that is, the billions of dollars he has extracted from his people and arranged to be stashed in dozens of banks all over the world, a hedge fund against the disasters that have happened to Mubarak in Egypt and Gaddafi in Libya. To simplify his task and Gabriel's, Silva posits that there is one man who controls and manages this vast financial empire, Walid al-Siddiqui, and that his records are stored in a single notebook always carried in the breast pocket of his jacket. It is a small step from this information to a plan to steal the notebook and get computer access to the multifarious accounts. But how is this to be done? Alas, it involves recruiting yet another young woman, Al-Siddiqui's secretary, who, like all of Allon's female recruits, will be put in extreme danger and only rescued at the last moment by way of a dubious deal between Allon and Assad's deputies, whereby he will trade her life (and a lifetime of well-financed security for her) for the billions of dollars he and his team have "confiscated" by sophisticated use of the Internet and will now electronically return. So what was all that effort for? Worse: Gabriel could have settled for the eight billion dollars of his first heist and removed his girl from danger, but he has become greedy. He sends her on a perilous mission into enemy territory to collect documents that he surmises will contain more information about Assad's finances.

"Isn't eight billion dollars enough?" she asked after a moment. "It's a great deal of money, Jihan, but I want more." "Why?" "Because it will allow us to have more influence over his actions" (p. 410). In the end, he has no money and no influence. This sounds like a moral fable worthy of Chaucer rather like *The Pardoner's Tale*.

Amedeo Modigliani, *Woman with a Fan* (1919). Musée d'art modern de Ia ville de Paris. Photo: Bulloz. © RMN-Grand Palais / Art Resource, NY.

Yet *The Heist* does offer some serious, and seriously needed today, historical information on Syria and its Alawite rulers, starting with the tyrannical father who emerged from a village via the war with Israel to become President in 1970 (pp. 263–265) and was most notorious for completely destroying the town of Hama, a hotbed of the Muslim Brotherhood, in 1982, creating a permanent warning known as Hama Rules. It was from Hama that Gabriel's brave female recruit, Jihan, emerged, having lost all the members of her family. In a 1991 presidential plebiscite, warned by Hama Rules, Assad's people elected him with 99.9 percent of the vote. And when he was succeeded by his middle son, the Arab Spring occurred, turning what had looked at first like a benign governmental change of tone into the civil war that has now lasted six years and decimated the country's population. Silva offers only a sketch, a hint intended surely to drive us to the Internet for more information. We will be appalled. But even in 2014 when *The Heist* was published, the "Author's Notes" could tell us, had to tell us, the scale of this holocaust:

> *More than 150, 000 people have been killed and another two million have been left homeless or have fled to neighboring countries . . . The number of Syrians living as refugees is soon expect to surpass four million, which would make it the largest refugee population in the world. Such is the legacy of four and a half decades of Assad family rule. If the slaughter and dislocation continues apace, the Assads might one day be rulers of a land without people (p. 496).*

Too bad Gabriel ruined his bargaining position by overreach.

THE NOT-SO-COLD WAR

THE NOT-SO-COLD WAR

Now we can turn back to the two novels we overrode in creating the Allon Saudi Arabia series. These books titled *Moscow Rules* (2008) and *The Defector* (2009) share several new and memorable characters, especially the endearing Russian defector, Grigori Bulganov, who saves the life of Gabriel and others and is briefly rewarded with a pleasant and supposedly protected life in London. Unfortunately, it is not sufficiently protected as we shall see. *Moscow Rules* is the first half of this tightly plotted Russian series in which Gabriel is sent to Moscow to prepare the way for the extraction of Elena Kharkov and her two children, not only from her country but also from her utterly criminal husband, Ivan Kharkov. *The Defector* records Ivan's revenge, which nearly takes the life not only of Gabriel but also of his wife, Chiara, kidnapped from their Italian villa and taken to Russia as a pawn. *The Defector* begins with the story of how Gabriel, quietly restoring a painting in the villa, is dragged back to deal with the disappearance from the London streets of Grigori, who is at first assumed by the British to have redefected back to Russia, a convenient explanation that would have absolved them from the responsibility from doing anything about it.

The premise of these two novels is that the Cold War is by no means over, although its manifestations, which were famously the territory of Silva's famous predecessor, John Le Carré, are quite different; perhaps not quite. Since these novels were written, their warnings have become more timely. President Putin's determination to rebuild the Soviet State is not only suspected but also documented by his own statements. The invasion of the Crimea and the partial invasion of the Ukraine, both in 2014, have given the Baltic States shudders. Military maneuvers by Russian planes and ships have been, to say the least, provocative. Silva's two Russian novels preceded these events, and the sins for which Putin's Russia is condemned therein are not invasions of territory but of press freedoms and human rights. Both these novels contain "Author's Notes" pointing to the repressive legislation Putin has put in place, including in 2008 a huge expansion of what constitutes treason (*The Defector*, p. 500). *Moscow Rules* declares that Russia has become "the third deadliest country in the world in which to practice the craft of journalism" (p. 502).

The long arm of the Kremlin does not only threaten journalists *within* Russia. The poisoning of Alexander Litvinenko and his death in November 2006 might very well have been one of the catalysts for *The Defector*, since Litvinenko was himself a defector from Russia who requested and received political asylum in Britain—actually as he arrived in Heathrow Airport—and in October 2006, one month before his murder, achieved British citizenship. Litvinenko's case is mentioned in *Moscow Rules* as an example of the heating up of Russian espionage activities in London to "levels not seen since the end of the Cold War" (p. 191). He had asked for asylum in the United States but had been refused. His presence in London makes a much better story for Silva, not least because he was working for the UK security service, M16. Like Grigori Bulganov, he refused to hide even in plain sight and even worked with Berezovsky in open protest against Putin's government. He alleged that the 1999 bombing of the apartment buildings, blamed on Chechen terrorists as a pretext for the second Chechen war, was actually coordinated by the FSB, the successor to the KBG, as also was the Russian theater hostage crisis. There were three other Russians who believed this, including the female journalist Anna Politkovskaya, who were soon assassinated. In his Author's Notes to *Moscow Rules*, Silva states that Politkovskaya was "gunned down in the elevator of her Moscow apartment house in October 2006" (p. 502), a month before Litvinenko's poisoning; and she may have been one of the truths behind Olga Sukhova, the reporter from *Moskovskaya Gazeta*, who knows the dark secrets of Ivan Karkhov. Olga, however, climbs the stairs with Gabriel to her eleventh-floor apartment and survives the shooters waiting on the landing. Since none of Silva's novels is a right-out tragedy, she will eventually be safely flown out of Russia.

This makes Silva's first two "Russian" novels rather closer to truth than fiction and to grave truth at that. But there is a third Silva novel that deals with Russia, *The English Girl*, which came out in 2013, and tackles another version of Putin's imperial aims: the creation of an international oil empire. A new company, Volgatek Oil and Gas, "was to have no role in domestic Russian oil production, which had already leveled off":

> *Instead, its sole purpose was to expand Russia's oil and gas interests internationally, thus increasing the Kremlin's global power and influence. Backed by Kremlin money, Volgatek went on a shopping spree in Europe, purchasing a chain of oil refineries in Poland, Lithuania, and Hungary. Then, over the objections of the Americans, it signed a lucrative drilling agreement with the Islamic Republic of Iran. It also signed development deals with Cuba, Venezuela, and Syria . . . All in the lands of the old Soviet empire or in countries hostile to the United States* (p. 307).

This is the report of a Russian business man, Victor Orlov, once in control of a large oil industry but now himself a defector in wealthy retirement in London and a vicious critic of Putin. In his view, the new Russian imperialism will be affected by international acquisitions of oil fields. In the novel's plot, its most recent attempt at conquest was in the North Sea off the coast of Britain, which design involves bribery, blackmail, and kidnapping of an English Girl. Note that we are still short of 2014, the year in which Putin turned to more traditional plans (invasion) for rebuilding great old Russia and which Silva has so far not tackled.

There is, thus, a Russian series here to balance the three Holocaust novels and the three Middle Eastern-Saudi ones. Now while it is not difficult to determine how much of the Holocaust series is based on fact (much of it) and why the Middle Eastern Series requires for its credibility some facts, such as the history of Waahabism or the failing development of Saudi Arabia, that problem is much more demanding here. "The Russian energy company known as Volgatek Oil and Gas does not exist" (p. 522), writes Silva blithely. Well, no. But what does exist is the Russian energy company known as Rosneft, which calls itself "the world's largest public oil company" and "carries out its activities in Belarus, Ukraine, Kazakhastan, Turkmenistan, China, Vietnam, Mongolia, Germany, Italy, Norway, Algeria, Brazil, Venezuela, UAE, and Armenia" (Rosneft's own website). The Russian government currently owns 75 percent of Rosneft's shares, although there is talk of increasing the amount owned by others (privatization!). When Daniel Silva copyrighted *The English Girl* in 2013, he could not have known that in May 2015, according to *The Economist*, the British Government tried to block a Russian investment in the North Sea. But as so often, it seems that Silva was ahead of the curve.

Each of these three novels has a painting for Gabriel to work on though the work may be interrupted. In *Moscow Rules*, it is the grisly rendering of the *Martyrdom of St. Erasmus* by Nicholas Poussin that shows the saint being disemboweled, his entrails wound out of his body onto a ship's capstan. The painting belongs to the Vatican. In *The Defector*, it is *The Crucifixion of St. Peter* by Guido Reni, a strange imitation and correction of Caravaggio's version of the same scene, still in the Church of San Paolo alle tre Fontane in Rome. Gabriel had gone back to Rome to absorb the Caravaggio to understand Reni's changes, which were masterly and moving. In *The English Girl*, the painting is about another kind of cruelty by men toward women as represented by Jacopo Bassano's *Susanna and the Elders* now in the Musée des Beaux-Arts, Reims, France. I will not strain the significance of these paintings, but it is important to note both their grimness, their representations of human vileness, as compared to earlier restoration projects for Gabriel, as also the fact that all three exist and can be seen today. This darkening of the art historical analogies, for this is what the paintings must at some level be, to the other jobs awaiting Gabriel, should not be ignored, nor should the remarkable effort of Daniel Silva to find and visit the paintings appropriate to his intentions, especially the third. But I would be reprimanded if I failed to point out that *Moscow Rules* also contains *another* painting, absolutely different in tone from all of the above: Mary Cassat's *Children Playing on the Beach*, marginally concealed by Silva's pseudonym, *Two Children on a Beach*. Innocence and sweetness incarnate. Significantly, most men regard Cassat's work as kitsch. Women love it. This fact allows Silva to use the painting, whose "real" version is in the National Gallery of Art in Washington, as a lure. It also says something about famous paintings, that they can be copied and forged.

Moscow Rules

It is appropriate that the Cassat takes on plot value in *Moscow Rules* since this is a novel about two young children who are themselves bones of contention between their parents, Ivan Karkhov, a Russian thug and arms dealer, and his gentle wife, Elena, who will knowingly purchase a fake version of the Cassat, forged by Gabriel, as a way of communicating her desire to be rid of her husband. The story begins, however, in a very different tone with Gabriel being called to Rome (away from a truly horrible painting of an evisceration) to meet and supposedly debrief a Russian journalist who has specifically asked to speak to him. Boris Ostrovsky is the second Russian journalist to attempt this communication, the first, Alexander Lubin, having been already assassinated in the south of France. Boris will be poisoned in an instant in his attempt to meet Gabriel on Vatican territory, and thus the theme of the Vatican in Gabriel's life and his almost familial relationship with the imaginary and admirable pope reemerges in the Russian series. The third endangered journalist is Anna Sukhova, described above; and Ostrovsky's death will require Gabriel, for the first time in his life, to visit Russia. There will be two more such visits.

The brilliantly ambiguous title of the novel (two nouns or the shortest possible sentence) does not, though it could, refer to Putin's style of government. It is a reference to Silva's most brilliant predecessor, John Le Carré, and his Cold War spy novels, especially *Smiley's People*. The rules were developed to be used *against* Russia during the Cold War, and Gabriel's team has been using some of them all along. They were designed to assist spies in not being spied upon, and they are governed by the term "tradecraft," which covers all kinds of tips for conducting surveillance and avoiding it. Some of them, especially the first, are quite philosophical. Here is the list as given in the International Spy Museum in Washington, D.C.:

1. *Assume nothing.*
2. *Never go against your gut.*
3. *Everyone is potentially under opposition control.*
4. *Don't look back: you are never completely alone.*
5. *Go with the flow; blend in.*
6. *Vary your pattern.*
7. *Lull them into a sense of complacency.*
8. *Don't harass the opposition.*
9. *Pick the time and place for action.*
10. *Keep your options open.*

And then there is always Murphy's Rule: "What can go wrong, will go wrong, and at the worst possible moment." Not an aspect of tradecraft as such, Murphy's Rule is an attitude.

It is, of course, no accident that the Moscow Rules fail completely at the outset of *Moscow Rules*. The Russian journalist Boris Ostrovsky had requested a personal meeting with Gabriel in the Vatican Basilica; and Eli Lavon, the team's best operator of tradecraft, has been watching him all afternoon to make sure he is not followed, that is, "clean." But the assassin uses one Moscow Rule to trump another. He followed Gabriel, not Ostrovsky, the watcher watching the watcher; and both arrived at the Basilica *before* the prey. Ostrovsky dies, struggling to breathe, just after a man in the crowd brushes against his arm. Gabriel figures the assassin injected a Russian poison that was developed by the KBG during the Cold War and shuts down the respiratory system immediately. Naturally, Gabriel is sent to Russia to attempt to learn the message Ostrovsky had tried to deliver. Using a false passport, an alias, Natan Golani, and attendance at a UNESCO conference as his excuse for being in St. Petersburg, Gabriel makes contact with Olga Sukhova and learns from her what she has learned from her friend Elena Karkhov. The ominous message is that an arms dealer with close ties to the Kremlin and Putin himself was about to conclude a major deal "that would put some very dangerous weapons into the hands of some very dangerous people" (p. 113), Al-Qaeda, or an affiliate. The arms dealer is, of course, Ivan Karkhov, who will also be the villain in *The Defector* and who also lives part time in London with

Mary Cassatt, *Children Playing on the Beach* (1884). National Gallery of Art, Washington, Ailsa Mellon Bruce Collection 1970.17.19.

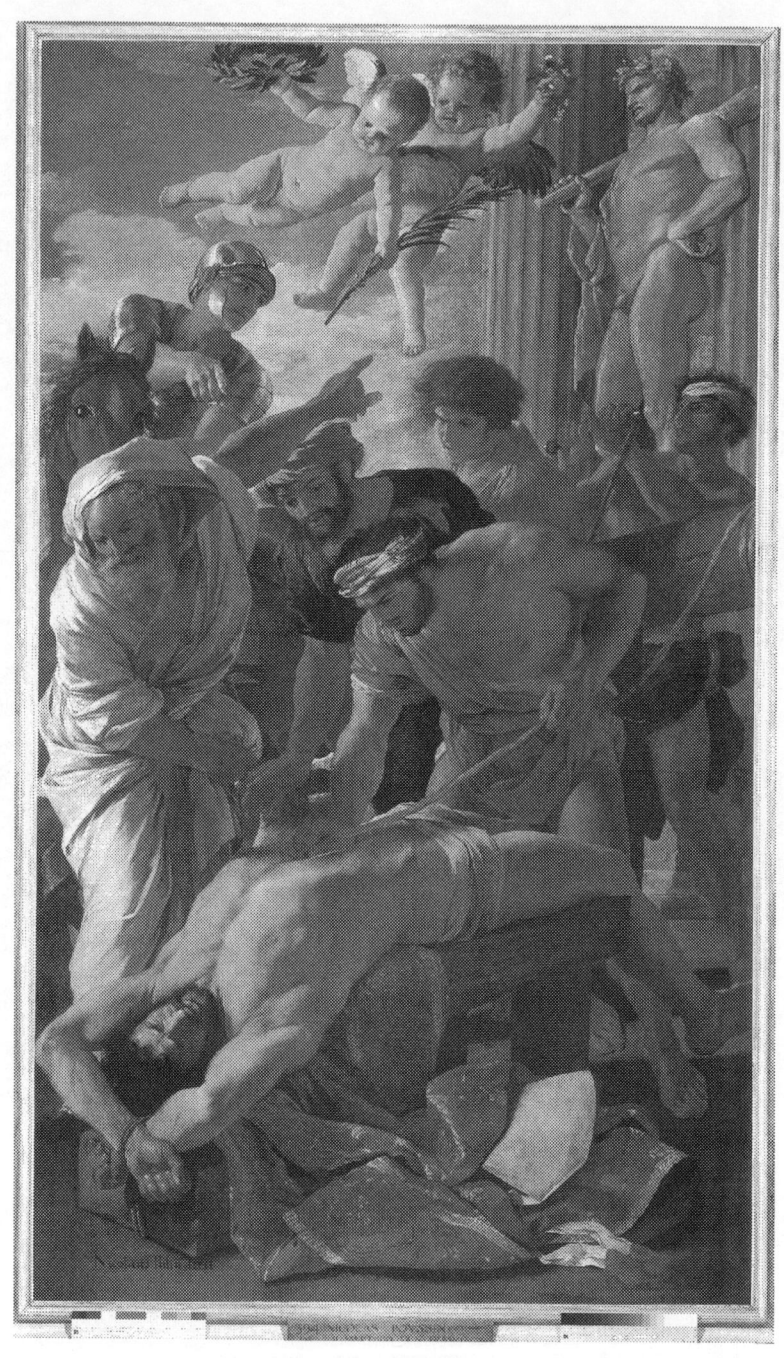

Nicolas Poussin, *The Martyrdom of Saint Erasmus* (1629). Pinacoteca,
Vatican Museums. Photo courtesy Scala / Art Resource, NY.

Elena and their two children, twins, a boy and a girl. Gabriel's first visit to Russia ends badly (for him), and it could have been far worse if not for the intervention of a mysterious Sergei, who gets him out of the Lubyanka and Russia into the Ukraine.

This is where the Cassat painting of *Two Children on a Beach* (as Silva frugally renames it) becomes an agent of an extremely complex plot to get access to Elena. I will say no more. Following it is extra fun because there is a cameo appearance of the engaging Sir John Boothby, son of the Sir Basil Boothby who saved the day in *The Unlikely Spy*, Silva's first venture in espionage fiction. It also involved the reappearance of Sarah, who will sell Elena a painting she desires and will shortly turn up in St. Tropez with Mikhail as her pretended lover to insinuate herself into the Karkhov household. Once enrolled into the plot against her husband, whom she now hates, Elena has to perform the most dangerous task in the entire story, getting hold of her husband's records. So Gabriel's second visit to Russia is to give her protection and backup. "What can go wrong will go wrong"; and it does, in part, because Gabriel is driving an inferior car. *Not* a very good example of tradecraft. And once more, the mysterious Sergei has to rescue them both. In return for which, he becomes, under their auspices, a defector. Gabriel arrives home with a seriously damaged and bandaged eye, and it will take weeks before the bandage can be removed and his sight assessed.

Nevertheless, one would have to say it was all worth it. The information that Elena steals from her husband's safe identifies the locations from which the "Arrows of Allah" will be launched and averts a worldwide terrorist disaster. More importantly, the evidence identifies their source—Ivan Karhov. "His assets were quickly seized, his bank accounts quickly frozen" (p. 487). Slinking back to Moscow, his presence there being stoutly denied by the Kremlin, he was caught on camera attending a Kremlin reception for the recently reelected Putin, accompanied by his stunning young new wife, Yekaterina, the supermodel, proof of whose existence had helped to recruit Elena Karkhov to Gabriel's team.

THE DEFECTOR

Ivan Karkhov did not stay in geopolitical exile very long. *Moscow Rules*, being finished in March 2008 and copyrighted in 2009, was promptly followed by its sequel in 2009. Not even Le Carré could bring out a book a year or sooner. The first chapter of *The Defector* is dated January; and in the "Author's Notes" there is a reference to the assassination of Stanislav Markelov, "crusading human rights lawyer," gunned down in a Moscow street in January 2009. The internal dating is tighter still. "The previous summer," we are told on page 138, Mikhail and Sarah Bancroft had infiltrated Kharkov's entourage, suggesting that Ivan had wasted very little time in exacting his revenge, which has two parts: the retrieval of the defector Grigori from the streets of London and the capture of Chiara from the summer villa in Italy, where the couple had been enjoying a brief respite from the demands of Gabriel's second career (or is it his first?). It is actually only Gabriel and his sharp eyes who can deduce that Grigori's sudden departure is not a redefection but a very clever kidnapping involving the passive cooperation of Grigori's wife, who still works in a travel agency in Moscow. And therefore he has the support of Adrian Carter on behalf of the British government, which does not like its hostages to international fortune to be stolen back. Naturally, this throws into question the security and status of Elena Kharkov and her twins, whom Gabriel will deploy in what, to me, is a completely unacceptable swap—two children for Chiara and Grigori—in an operation that is entirely unbelievable and only half successful. In the unsuccessful half, Grigori is killed; and what is worse, his corpse is taken back to London and dumped in the streets. Chiara is rescued, barely. The Kharkov children stay safely in the United States.

Guido Reni, *The Crucifixion of Saint Peter* (1605). Pinacoteca, Vatican Museums. Photo courtesy Nimatallah / Art Resource, NY.

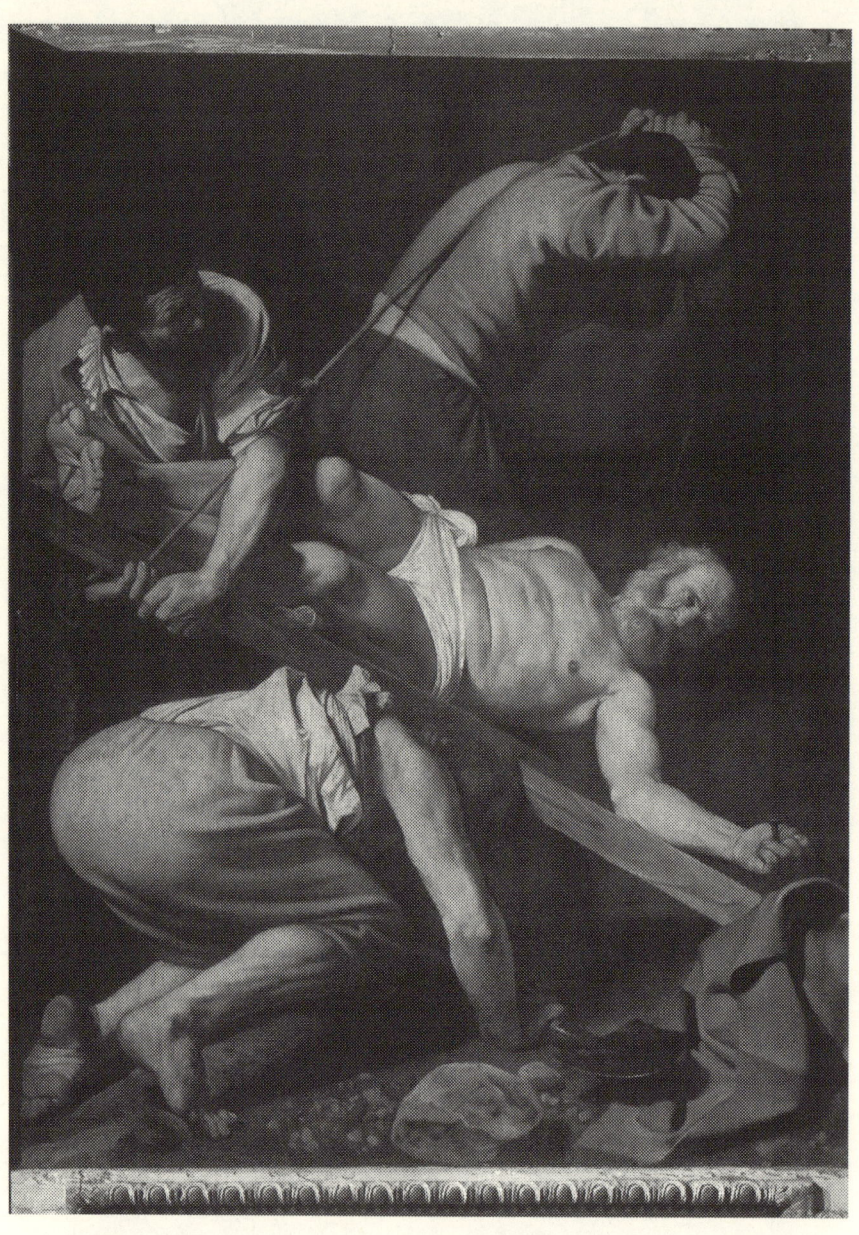

Caravaggio, *Crucifixion of Saint Peter* (1600-1601). Cerasi Chapel, Santa
Maria del Popolo, Rome. Photo courtesy Scala / Art Resource, NY.

And the point of the novel seems not to be these powerfully personal events but the discovery that Ivan has inherited a dachau used by Stalin to dispose of his victims in mass graves. Now that is credible though fictional. And Silva explains his motivation in the "Author's Notes," where he tells of visiting a comparable site of mass graves in Butovo, just south of Moscow, where Russian citizens can publicly mourn their deplorable history (p. 500). I am not sure this is quite enough to justify the sequel in both senses of the word "justify." But the third "Russian" novel may push these doubts to the back of the mind.

THE ENGLISH GIRL

In his third Russian novel, *The English Girl* (2013), Gabriel participates in an elaborate plot to unveil the dastardly story of Volgatek Oil and Gas and its ambitions to make off with the contents of the North Sea oil fields. In this novel, Gabriel works only in a secondary capacity to his more endangered teammate from the Office, Mikhail Abramov, who will pose as a young and rising oil executive to infiltrate Volgatek. Gabriel's job is to ensure Mikhail's safety and, accidentally, to find the eponymous "English Girl" who has caused so much trouble in Britain, and bring her home; not that it is her "real" home, for she has none. The discovery that she is alive and well in St. Petersburg, spending every day in the Hermitage, contemplating a painting by Manet, *The Pond at Montgeron*, allows Gabriel to solve two problems at once: the rescue of another endangered maiden (long thought murdered) and the exposure of the plot to gain access to the North Sea oil fields, which involved the all too human failings of the British Prime Minister. The Prime Minister (who is clearly not the even more unfortunate David Cameron) took the allegorically named Madeline Hart, who is really a Russian girl posing as an English girl, as his mistress and then, when her abduction was announced and a massive ransom demanded, paid the ransom and dropped his objections to the Volgatek coup. But the chief villain behind the scenes was his right-hand man, Jeremy Fallon, who himself had taken a huge bribe to arrange the whole affair. I refrain from telling what happens in the end, although I may already have said too much. Think about Manet's painting as being an especially beautiful form of closure, comparable in its message to the quietly playing children of Mary Cassat, that is, a closure preferable to

Claude Monet, *Pond at Montgeron* (c. 1876). State Hermitage
Museum. Image is used from www.hermitagemusum.org, courtesy
of The State Hermitage Museum, St. Petersburg, Russia.

the usual Silva wrap-up of the villains, which also occurs here and can be skipped if you prefer.

The quietly playing children of Mary Cassat. It is extremely clever of Daniel Silva to end *The English Girl* not with Madeline Hart, who will have to be stashed somewhere safe and hence very lonely (Gabriel volunteers his Cornwall cottage), but with Chiara on Corsica, learning from the old *signadora*, who has summoned her in the village that she is, at last, pregnant again. She had lost a baby in Russia and had difficulty conceiving subsequently. But after the old woman has put her to the magic test of the drop of oil in the water, she says, "Go home and tell [your husband] he's going to be a father again." "Boy or girl?" asks Chiara. "The old woman smiled and said, 'One of each'" (p. 520).

But what I have completely failed to mention so far is a powerful new ingredient in the Gabriel Allon world: a figure whom we have actually met before without paying much attention. We met him as "the English Assassin," who was sent to kill Gabriel and his famous musician friend in that novel but who apparently had a fit of conscience and left his targets unharmed. "In Venice, in another lifetime" (p. 77). This was Christopher Keller, a professional assassin now employed by Don Orsati but who agrees to join forces with Gabriel in the attempt to find Madeline Hart. They make a great team, and Silva's style extends to offering us banter exchanged between the two men that lightens the tone. As in, staring at the pouring rain in Marseilles with no sign of their prey, Keller says, "Maybe we should get a hotel room." And Gabriel replies, "It's a bit soon for that, don't you think. After all, we've only just met."

Keller is a dead man, or so the English authorities and his elderly parents have been led to believe. Technically, he is a deserter from the British military; but in 1990, he was the only survivor of a dreadful attack of friendly fire in the Iraqi desert, and there was nothing left to desert from:

> *His first instinct was to radio his base and request an extraction. Instead, enraged by the incompetence of his superiors, he started walking . . . made his way through the Coalition forces, and slipped undetected into Syria. From there, he hiked westward across Turkey, Greece and Italy until he finally washed ashore in Corsica, where he fell into the waiting arms of Don Orsati . . . who gave him work. With his northern European looks and*

> *SAS training, Keller was able to fulfil contracts [to kill] that were far beyond the capabilities of Orsati's Corsican-born Taddunaghiu (assassins)* (p. 75).

All this background information makes Keller bad but not absolutely bad and certainly capable of being "restored" by Gabriel though not yet, not until the end of *The English Spy* (2015), which was initially thought of, I shall argue, as the end of the Gabriel Allon series. *The English Assassin*, *The English Girl*, and *The English Spy* therefore form yet another silver thread in the Silva canvas.

Why did Silva write *The English Girl*, whose title tells us nothing about the book's "real" subject, which is the Russian oil industry and its connections to Vladimir Putin? Answering this question requires us to troll through the really heavy and discouraging material that Silva has stuffed into his novel. Indeed, it requires exposition by a Russian villain, Pavel Zhirov, who explains it all after an intense experience of torture by icy water. The exposition takes us back to the end of the Soviet Union in December 1991 when not only did the country crumble into fifteen separate states but the KGB collapsed and was reconstructed into two units as well, one of which was the SVR, the same service under a different name. Zhirov was named the SVR's new chief *resident* in Washington but was then redirected by the new president, Putin himself, to take charge of a new imperative:

> *[Zhirov] reminded his audience that, for decades, the Soviet Union was the world's second largest oil producer, trailing only Saudi Arabia and the emirates of the American-dominated Persian Gulf . . . The new Russian president understood what Boris Yeltsin had not, that oil could turn Russia into a superpower again. So he showed the oligarchs like Victor Orlov the door and brought the entire Russian energy sector under effective Kremlin control. And then he started an oil company of his own . . . We were tasked with acquiring drilling rights and downstream assets outside Russia* (p. 439).

"Whose idea was it to drill in the North Sea?"

It was his. He took it very personally. He said he wanted Volgatek to stick a straw into British territorial water, and suck on it until there was nothing left . . . He called me into his Kremlin office and told me to use all and any means necessary to get that contract (p. 440).

This information, with only slightly less colorful language, is repeated by Silva in his "Author's Note" to the novel:

Stripped of its empire and militarily feeble, Russia now intends to wield power on the world stage with oil and gas rather than nuclear weapons and Marxist–Leninist ideology . . . In Russia, the steady descent into authoritarianism continues. And the Kremlin's oil and gas giants are footing the bill (p. 527).

The thin skin between fact and fiction in Silva's novels is sometimes very thin indeed, and the message of this one is clearly beware of Putin, whom we can expect to be in power until at least 2024 (p. 525).

IRELAND

How Not To Say
Good-Bye: The
English Spy

In 1893, thousands of English readers canceled their subscription to *The Strand* when Sherlock Holmes fell off a cliff and died. Sir Arthur Conan Doyle was so taken aback by this reaction that he created another Holmes novel, *The Adventure of the Empty House*, to appease his public. It was a prequel. It just gave the audience a bit more Holmes. Later, it appeared that he had survived the fall! These events illuminate the predicament of the novelist who succeeds so well in creating a series featuring one exceptional protagonist that people mourn his disappearance and blame the author for ruining their recreation. As I remarked in the Introduction, the greatest problem with a series such as this is that the "realism" effect for which most novelists strive requires that the protagonist must age.

John Le Carré anticipated this problem as soon as he realized he had a potential series on his hands by revising the timeline of George Smiley's early life, having him enter the Intelligence business in 1937, not 1928, presumably so that his "realistically" advancing age would not conflict with the "realism" effect of his subsequent appearances. He also had Smiley retire twice in his career. In March 2010, Le Carré told an audience at the Sheldonian Theater in Oxford that Smiley would now be "very old and getting past [it]—certainly his nineties." Le Carré envisaged his character as "still alive but very much retired, keeping bees somewhere." In 2015, the film *Mr. Holmes* seems to have merged Le Carré's comment with Sir Conan Doyle's dilemma since the central character, played chillingly by Ian McKellan, is clearly very old, indeed; retired with creeping dementia; and keeping bees. So far, the hero of Lee Child's series, the Jack Reacher novels, has neither died nor retired nor discovered a serious hobby; but his author has kept the problem of aging tantalizingly in our thoughts by turning it into a puzzle for the reader to solve. I have described this puzzle elsewhere. In *The Killing Floor*, Reacher is thirty-six years old; and in *Make Me*, the last of the series so far, he must be fifty-two or fifty-three. This is more of a problem with a character who fights with his brawn (and has a *very* active sex life) than for Smiley, who only uses his brain. There is no indication as yet as to what Child intends to do with him; but he has produced a prequel, *Night School*, in which Reacher is still in the army and only thirty-five.

The English Spy is the last novel in the Gabriel Allon series, which is just as well since Allon is now, if we have been keeping track, in his early sixties. To be precise, in *The Confessor*, "he had recently celebrated his fifty-first birthday" (p. 33), and that was twelve years after 1991, that is, 2003. Chiara is twenty years younger. In the Silva calendar, *The English Spy* occurs twelve years later, that is, 2015. Gabriel must be sixty-three. He is finally out of the assassination business and after three months of paternity leave will be formally installed as Chief of the Israel Office. He has abandoned his painter's cottage in Gunwalloe Cove, Cornwall. He has arranged for Keller, who is ten years younger, to work for Graham Seymour in his place. His twins are about to be born, rounding off the sad tale of Dani in the best possible way. But is it really the end of the series? In the "Author's Note," Silva writes teasingly that there will be more news of Gabriel "in the next installment of the series" (p. 519). One hopes not for the following reasons:

The English Spy announces itself as some sort of successor to *The English Assassin* and *The English Girl*. The most obvious connection is with *The English Assassin*, a role self-chosen by Christopher Keller (Killer), who failed to complete his mission to eliminate Gabriel and his famous violinist, Anna Rolfe, way back in 2002. In this novel, the term "spy" does penance for "assassin," although some of the jobs assigned to Keller when he comes out of exile to work for the British security forces will include assassination. This ethical transfer and obfuscation is never discussed by Silva, although

Paolo Veronese, *Madonna and Child in Glory above Saint Sebastian* (1562). Chancel of Saint Sebastiano, Venice. Photo courtesy Scala I Art Resource, NY.

I suspect that many of his readers will be satisfied not to think too deeply about it, having witnessed one of the most emotional scenes in the Allon series, the return of Keller to his elderly parents who have believed him dead all these years:

> *His parents stood in the entrance hall, disbelieving of their eyes. Keller raised a finger to his lips and gathered them into his powerful arms before quickly closing the door . . . Then a shade fell and he was gone* (p. 494).

It is hard to do closure any better than this. But actually, Silva does it better a few pages later when Gabriel, back in Narkiss Street with his wife just about to deliver their twins, asks if he may redo the clouds she has painted in the children's nursery, obliterating her work as too "childish":

> *He swiftly decorated the wall in a bank of glowing Titianesque clouds. Lastly he added a small child angel, a boy, who was peering downward over the edge of the highest cloud on the scene below. The scene was borrowed from Veronese's Virgin and Child and Glory with the Saints. With tears in his eyes and a trembling hand, the face of his son as it appeared on the night of his death. Then he signed his name and the date and it was done* (pp. 506–507).

Lovely in its thought and the immortalization of Dani but not quite accurate as an account of this painting, alas. The boy peering down over the edge of the cloud, mentioned by Richard Cocke in his study of Veronese—and it is a striking pictorial statement about the two realms, heavenly and earthly—does not show us his face. Silva's memory of it must have failed him. Or could the inaccuracy perhaps be Gabriel's last act of pictorial restoration? In fact, in this novel, there has been no real painting for Gabriel to rescue.

But these are aesthetic or organizational forms of closure. And they pull in the opposite direction from the most traditional closure: death. Killing off your protagonist is generally frowned upon by those who advise fiction writers how to get out of a novel or novels, and it is especially a bad idea of kill off someone on whom readers have come to rely. Even worse is resurrection, which can be seen as cheesy even when the death is later revealed not to have been fatal. Gabriel's decision, to declare that he had died in the bombing outside Harrods, is not exactly cheesy; but it certainly stretches credulity, especially as his wounds are patched up by a private doctor without hospitalization. Yes, there is a reason for it in terms of the hunt for Eamon Quinn. But it causes immense pain to those who loved him—Sarah, Leah, Julian Isherwood, the Pope. It seems as though the heavily pregnant Chiara must have been let in on the secret, but this we are never told.

This novel provokes more questions than it answers, not the least of which is why Silva chose to start it with an undeniable bang—the murder of an ex-princess who is carefully given a biography comparable to that of Princess Diana—while denying that this event has an historical basis. Why kill the princess off again, especially since she has been dead since 1997, nearly twenty years? What version of the truth/fiction dialectic is Silva playing with here? Why on earth would President Putin, if looking for revenge against Gabriel for scotching his plans to drain oil from the North Sea for his own company, try such a devious approach? Looking more closely, how did Eamon Quinn, *if* at the behest of Putin, learn that she would be taking this cruise, a question Gabriel himself asks, which remains steadfastly unanswered (p. 60)? Of course, Quinn *could* have been in constant communication with Putin while he was waiting in Gustavia for something to happen. Perhaps he even arranged for the honey trap that lured away Spider Barnes, the usual chef of the *Aurora*, the fatal yacht, and possibly disposed of him too. But how could he have known in advance that, after trying several other restaurants, he would be hired as a chef at Le Piment, whose chef had stormed off that very day in a dispute over wages? This is really pushing "luck" or coincidence further than most readers, if reading carefully, would be prepared to swallow.

Pushing credibility further, could Putin be sure that it would be Gabriel who would be dispatched by British Intelligence—i.e., Graham Seymour—to track Quinn down? How plausible is it that the discovery of half a tram ticket in a girl's bedroom in Ireland would lead Gabriel to Lisbon and from there to Quinn's flat, where his accomplice was waiting on a balcony to lead them to Heathrow and thence to Brompton Road, where Gabriel would become a victim of the bomb that Quinn had arranged to have deposited outside Harrods? And how likely is it that Gabriel, who threw himself back into the fireball created by Quinn, survived when the car whose occupants he was trying to rescue was vaporized? Incredulity reins. Okay, so it's a novel. But Silva's previous novels have not stretched our trust so far.

And then there is the convergence of plots, for, it seems, the assassination of the princess is not at all a main plot to be followed to its conclusion but merely an attention-getting device. The main plot or plots send Gabriel and Keller *twice* into modern-day Ireland, modern but still reeking with the aftermath of the Troubles: the first time to try and find clues to the whereabouts of Quinn, the second time to rescue our English Girl, Madeline Hart, who has been kidnapped from Gabriel's beloved cottage in Cornwall (lent to her for her safety after *The English Girl* draws to its quite satisfactory close). The cottage, imagined for us and Gabriel as painted by Claude Monet, doesn't turn out to be at all a safe haven. In fact, the bloodshed there ruins it as a place where Gabriel might in the future paint or restore. This plot ends in a fine shootout between Gabriel and Keller and die-hard Real IRAs, which predictably, the IRAs lose.

However, this is not the only main plot! Dubiously intertwined is yet another Iranian nuclear episode, including a Vevak informant (who survives because he smokes out the Russian, who does not) and the mysterious theft of "one hundred pounds of highly radioactive nuclear material . . . from a secret Iranian laboratory near the sacred city of Qom and sold on the black market to a smuggler linked to Chechen Islamic terrorists" (p. 324). Possibly since this is only a lure to get Alexei Rozanov into Gabriel's hands, we are never told whether the report is true; and if so, what happened to the dangerous stuff? Who cares? This is just another trick, using nuclear threat in a casual and frivolous manner.

All these questions and implied criticisms imply that I think Daniel Silva was running out of steam by the time he got to his fifteenth Allon novel. How many times, indeed, can you replay the same tricks with the same crew even if the country and/or the political scenario varies? How many physical disasters can Gabriel survive? He does spend a great deal of time over the series recuperating. How much time does the visibly deteriorating Shamron have? A novel without him would have a large hole in it. It was a smart move to recruit Christopher Keller to the cause since he is built as a killing machine and is, one must conclude, only in his early fifties by the time he gets his revenge for the Omagh bombings and the killing of his Irish sweetheart. It is possible that Silva is planning to use him to carry the series forward. But then we would miss the witty give and take between him and Gabriel, who surely must stay full time in the Office.

You can tell that I am having difficulty saying good-bye to this marvelous project. But I have an exit device of my own, which is to review the "Author's Notes" and their very interesting and original function. Taking seriously (philosophically) the truth/fiction dichotomy, which Silva has challenged throughout by mixing them in persuasive ways, one could see the "Author's Notes" as partly a game, partly a theoretical intervention in the task of writing.

"The Author's Notes"

In later novels, these will appear at the end, helping the reader to sort through what she had just read; but in *The Kill Artist*, the first in the series, the equivalent appears at the beginning, taking the place of the very common disclaimers of reference to anyone living or dead. However, Silva adds, "In order to add verisimilitude . . . I have drawn from real episodes in the secret war between Israeli intelligence and the Palestinian guerillas. For instance, the 1998 assassination of PLO commando leader Abu Jihad happened much as it is portrayed, with minor modifications." That is rather coy. The "minor modifications" consisted in fitting Gabriel into the role actually played by one Nahum Lev, a Sayeret Matkal officer, who led the team after months of official planning and watching. Abu Jihad, whose real name was Al-Wazir, was indeed shot in his home in Tunis at close range in the presence of his wife and son. This fictional reassignment establishes Gabriel's credentials as an assassin, but it also haunts him, not least because he also comes face-to-face with Al-Wazir's daughter just after the shooting (pp. 149-151). It is much to the point that I am making here that the "real" story of the assassination was censored by Israel for more than a decade.

The other significant breach of truth admitted by Silva in this same disclaimer is the invention of the painting that Gabriel is asked to restore: Francesco Vecellio's *Adoration of the Shepherds* "does not exist." In the light of later novels, where the paintings are really real, one has to ask why. And why Vecellio anyway, always a minor painter in the shadow of his great brother Titian? But to use this imaginary painting, whose authentication depends on Julian Isherwood's acumen, raises the huge question of whether a painting is "really" by a particular artist, which in turn, in later novels, will lead to the question of why the "original" is worth so hugely much more than a copy so brilliant that one cannot tell the one from the other.

In *The English Assassin*, Silva's second Allon, the "afterword" does not address the truth/fiction issue directly. It simply reports on the factual basis for the claims made therein for the Nazi looting of works of art from the countries they occupied. "In 1996, the Swiss federal assembly created the so-called Independent Commission of Experts and ordered it to investigate the activities of Switzerland during the Second World War" (p. 435). After five years, the commission released its final report in the most general terms, acknowledging no blame. The ironic "so-called" points forward to *The Rembrandt Affair* and the really gripping story of one particular Rembrandt but which serves as the emotional center of a story of Nazi theft.

Moving right along, in *The Confessor*, his third Allon novel, Silva made historical truth and the right to investigate it his central idea. The theme of the novel is the role played by the Catholic Church and the papacy of Pope Pius XII in the Second World War—their hidden complicity, even alliance, with those who were planning to exterminate the Jews. After his opening disclaimer about the resemblance to any person, living or dead, being "entirely coincidental," Silver proceeds to direct us to Martin Luther (the second) and the Wannsee Conference, whose minutes are available for us to read. This inserts into the novel an uncomfortable nugget of documentary information as well as a plea for more openness. Before Silva created his fictional Pope, the Vatican remained intransigent with respect to the documents in its files, having released merely wartime diplomatic material, which naturally stymied the 1999 commission of independent historians supposedly convened to find out the truth. What they asked for—"diaries, memoranda, appointment books, minutes of meetings, draft documents"—and the personal papers of senior Vatican officials were not produced and probably never will be (p. 455).

This "Note" therefore directs our attention to another difficult aspect of truth in our times. Not only with respect to the Vatican, of course, but also in all dealings of and with senior government officials, CIA operatives, ministers, etc. How much secrecy is necessary for the normal operations of a state? How long should it be allowed to last? When should the curtains be undrawn? Can fiction do the work that the timid keepers of reputations refuse to do? In this case, I believe the answer is yes because

Silva's imaginary pope takes it upon himself to apologize to the Jews all over the world for the activities of one of his predecessors.

For *A Death in Vienna*, Silva sharpens his tone and, we might say, steps up to the plate. The "Author's Note" sounds a note of confidence we have not heard hitherto:

> *Heinrich Gross was indeed a physician at the notorious Spiegelgrund clinic . . . and the description of the halfhearted Austrian attempt to try him in 2000 is entirely accurate . . . Action 1005 was the real code name of the Nazi program to conceal evidence of the Holocaust . . . The leader of the operation, an Austrian named Paul Blobel [the original of Radek] . . . was convicted at Nuremberg for his role in the Einsatzgruppen mass murders and sentenced to death. Bishop Alois Hudal was indeed the rector of the Pontificio Santa Maria dell'Anima, and helped hundreds of Nazi war criminals flee Europe . . . The Vatican maintains that Bishop Hudal was acting without the approval or knowledge of the pope* (p. 420).

If you believe that, you'll believe anything. But that is the nature of belief. When we turn to *Prince of Fire*, the "Author's Note" becomes more forthright in its admission that its plot is "based on real events." "I borrowed much from Ali Hassan Salemeh . . . (the architect of the Munich Olympics Massacre) and his famous father to construct the fictional Asad and Sabri al-Khalifa" (p. 40). The image at the heart of the story is a real photograph of a boy sitting in the lap of Yasir Arafat (obviously a real person), who "fell ill and died," wrote Silva, "as I was completing this novel." The slender wall between fiction and news, between a novel and "real events," here comes tumbling down, not least since the "Note" ends by blaming Arafat for the terrorism that continues to rock the world. Yet it also admits that "Tochnit Dalet was the real name of the plan to remove hostile Arab population centers from land allocated for the new State of Israel" and that although the village of Beit Sayeed never existed, that of Sumayriyya did. If we read the novel as a statement of cautious sympathy for the Arab victims of Sumayriyya, the question of where blame should fall is open to debate.

In this respect, the penultimate novel, *The English Spy*, perhaps has a special claim on our attention since the "Author's Notes" have two very particular messages to deliver: one, that those responsible for the Omagh bombings, whose identities are well known, have been remarkably successful in avoiding conviction or, if convicted, paying the reparation demanded by the courts. Two, that the man really to be wary of in 2015 and hence today is not a Middle Eastern Tyrant or a wild Irishman but the meek-looking Vladimir Putin of Russia. His plans, according to Silva, are huge indeed:

> *Much has changed . . . since the collapse of the Soviet Union, but fomenting discord within the Western alliance remains a primary goal of Russia under Vladimir Putin . . . Under his leadership, Russia is once again quietly funneling money to extreme political parties in Western Europe on both the left and the right. It seems Putin doesn't care much about his friends' politics, so long as they are opposed to the United States* (p.523).

Gabriel Allon, Silva points out, first matched wits with Putin in 2008 "when Moscow was awash in oil revenues and critics of the Kremlin were being killed on the streets. Unfortunately, *the novel proved to be prescient.*" And Silva then listed Russia's recent behavior, including its support of Assad in Syria, its takeovers in Crimea and Eastern Ukraine, its bellicose aircraft maneuvers, and the fact that the terrorists who attacked the Istanbul airport in 2016 were Russian speakers. Gabriel has come a long way from the Jewish boy sent out by Golda Meir and Shamron to revenge an attack on Jewish athletes, and the widening gyre of Silva's fiction is itself a remarkable achievement. The critique of President Obama for dismissing Russia as a "regional power" that was acting out of weakness rather than strength (p. 524) will not be pertinent much longer. Let us hope that *The English Spy* is on the reading list of the new president of the United States or at least that someone puts on his desk its Author's farewell notes. If indeed he reads.

I am gradually making the claim that it is in the "Author's Notes" as they develop from one novel to another that Silva explains his own position and inserts a degree of didacticism and an increasingly tense relationship with real international politics as they unfold in real time. The notes get longer and, eventually, as in *The English Girl*, serve as independent essays. They greatly expand on the role of the novelist who deals with serious matters. They bring to the surface the uneasy standards of "relevance" or "topicality" as they have dogged the would-be novelist either as incentives or disincentives since Dickens. And, as I have asserted more than once, they establish the claim of Gabriel Silva, a claim he does not make for himself, for foreseeing, and advice based on prescience.

SYRIA

The Black Widow

Well, now it is finally out, the latest Silva novel. Can it be the final Silva novel? The problems I noted in my previous chapter (which has itself lost its status as a "last" chapter) are, if anything, exacerbated here. Gabriel is still (still) expected daily to take over the role of head of the Office from Uzi Navot. He is, of course, older still by at least a year. Therefore, he is sixty-four. Also, he seems to have shrunk. In *Prince of Fire*, he is five foot eight inches, there described as of "an unimpressive physical stature" (p. 28). But in *The Black Widow*, he sorely disappoints Christian Bouchard, who has been sent to meet him at Charles de Gaulle airport, as being "five foot nothing and maybe, *maybe*, a hundred and fifty pounds" (p. 70). I have to admit that on an earlier page (p. 42), Gabriel is registered as "below average in height—five foot eight, perhaps." So perhaps this is just a blooper. If so, it is a symptom of many aspects of this novel that are disturbing and finally unsatisfactory.

Gabriel is a man who refuses to retire, at least from his primary job, that of being one of the world's most famous and successful assassins. As I have demonstrated in previous chapters, it is possible to construct Gabriel's exact age from the various hints dropped by Silva. He must be sixty-four. Yet we are now told "his age was one of the most closely guarded secrets in Israel." "No verifiable date of birth ever found its way into print" (p. 42). This novel is set shortly before the first birthday of his twins, who, in the closing pages of *The English Spy*, were about to be delivered. The veil dropped over his age now is presumably to distract us from the specter of a man in his sixties starting a family. And from the fact that he is now taking on the most fearsome threat he has faced so far, the emergence out of the ruins of Al-Qaeda a larger and more ambitious enemy of the West, Isis or the soi-disant Islamic State. Is he up to it? As we shall see, the answer is no. I will postpone the inevitable question of judgment—why set him up to fail?—until my readers and Silva have experienced that failure.

The scope of this novel's challenge is far wider even than that of *Portrait of a Spy*, Silva's first extension of his landscape into the turbulent Middle East itself. Although some commentators who have been watching from a closer position might challenge Silva's view that the rise of Isis is more dangerous than threats from Al-Qaeda or any of the other extremist groups, this claim is made plausible by Silva's invention of a new leader who is truly a master mind and has assumed the name of the great medieval conqueror, Saladin. Saladin has truly imperialist aims:

> *He was no fire-breathing jihadist . . . His Islam was political rather than spiritual, a tool by which he intended to redraw the map of the Middle East. It would be dominated by a massive Suni state that would stretch from Baghdad to the Arabian Peninsula and across the Levant and North Africa. He did not rant or spew venom or recite Koranic verses of the Prophet. He was entirely reasonable, which made him all the more terrifying. The liberation of Jerusalem . . . was high on his agenda* (p. 317).

Thus he intended to reverse the First Crusade.

Saladin plans to rewrite history in the mode in which it had been written since the twelfth century when the original Saladin (Salah al-Din) defeated the Crusaders at the Battle of Hattin in 1187, paving the way for the Islamic reconquest of Jerusalem. It had been rewritten several times since then. But the new Saladin intends rolling back the great Persian carpet over the petty ambitions of missionaries, oil seekers, silly little nation states, or the even sillier grand American strategy of bending the Middle East to its own "strategic interests," the phrase used by President Jimmy Carter to justify the switch of American military resources to the Gulf area. I refer to the Carter Doctrine, announced in 1980 in response to the Soviet invasion of Afghanistan, and which thirty years later, Andrew Bacevich could, with reason, determine to be a shift in U.S. policy, "whose impact has been almost entirely pernicious." A late extension of the Cold War had reorganized the world so as to make the Middle East no longer a backwater but the *center* of international politics and American interventionalism. Among the consequences listed by Bacevich are the three wars in Afghanistan and the first, second, and third Iraq wars. And of course, the war in Syria in which Russia has played and is still playing a diabolic role—diabolic because Russia refuses to admit what it is doing.

Silva puts this straightforwardly in his "Author's Note," a feature of the novels that, as I have previously suggested, renders them uniquely qualified to straddle the truth/fiction border and, therefore, to have access to what frequently looks like prophecy. Here, he writes:

> *There is no doubt that the American invasion of Iraq in March 2003 created the seedbed from which Isis sprang. And there is also no doubt that the failure to leave a residual American force in Iraq, combined with the outbreak of civil war in Syria, allowed the group to flourish and spread on two sides of an increasingly meaningless border* (p. 522).

Just how meaningless it is, and has always been, has been an unpleasant discovery for Turkey, which feels threatened from the east as well as the Kurdish north. So the Cold War, completely unacknowledged, continues in a new slice of territory, meanwhile bringing unrest in those European countries that are still willing to accept Syrian refugees.

But Silva is now foretelling the shift in Islamic priorities from various European countries to America itself to the "homeland," as it preemptively likes to call itself, and in which various small squibs of violence have already gone off. In real time. Of course, they were not small to the victims; but at least, so far, they do not seem to be organized by a master mind. In the novel, they are. Saladin sees his agenda as being so deeply to wound America in its own territory that it would be lured out, to wage a "final apocalyptic battle in a place called Dabiq" (p. 485), which, of course, Isis would win. Hence, the terrorist attacks in Paris (the Weinberg Center) and Amsterdam (a bustling Jewish market) are merely warm-ups for a huge attack on Washington, D.C., the very heart of the "homeland." Ironically, during this multi-target operation, the National Counterterrorism Center was blown apart with Gabriel inside it. Naturally, Gabriel survives this, the "last" (?) of so many symbolic woundings, with only his hearing temporarily disrupted. It is not quite clear to me why Silva has returned to his theme of the resurgence of European anti-Semitism, serious though it be, but it does not fit smoothly into the larger story of an increasingly wide conflict between the East and the West.

But this grand international scenario is underwritten—and most of the novel is devoted to this diversion—by Gabriel's recruitment of yet another woman who will be deeply damaged by her involvement with him. That she is a Jew compelled to metamorphose into a Palestinian for the purpose of access to Saladin adds a level of psychological sophistication to this (final?) recruitment. Natalie Mizrahi is a young Jewish doctor living and practicing medicine in Israel. Her medical practice gives her an aura of righteousness that Gabriel's other female recruits do not have, and that rectitude both enables and complicates her duty when finally summoned to treat Saladin in Raqqa for what would otherwise have been mortal wounds. Whose side is she on? Initially, it seems that the recovering Saladin will be grateful enough to have her come and live with him in Damascus as his personal physician, his Maimonides. But in fact, she is to be deployed back in London as a suicide bomber, who only survives the complex plot because her suit of explosives fails to detonate.

There is a strong ambiguity as to how much of what happens to Natalie (now Leila Hadawi) is voluntary or involuntary. To begin with, she is virtually kidnapped from her apartment in Jerusalem by Gabriel's operative, Dina, who steals her personal letters and packs her suitcase for her with inadequate underwear. This invasion of her privacy is only the start of her humiliations. She is meekly a passenger in Dina's car as they drive to Gabriel's farm in the Jezreel Valley. Here, she is subjected to (verb highly intended) "the vetting, the probing, the inquisition" that is necessarily a part of her recruitment (p. 134). After weeks of intensive training, she is actually kidnapped and interrogated by three of Gabriel's men posing as Arabs. When she passes the test, Dina takes her to an apartment in Tel Aviv, where are spread out for her all the necessary French documents to send her back to France under her new name as well as an emerald-colored *hibab*, which is both the symbol and the technique of her transformation. First the *hibab* and later a heavy black *burqua* serve to disguise her. They also, of course, utterly subordinate her.

Once back in France, she is to run a brand-new general clinic in the dreary Northern Paris banlieue of Aubervilliers while watched over (for her safety) by French and Israeli secret servicemen. Much waiting follows, waiting for Saladin's operation to learn of her existence and suitability for the task. But eventually, she is approached and recruited for a visit to Raqqa, Syria, via Greece. She is accompanied, or rather directed, by another young woman, Amanda Ward, who is definitely working for the enemy. Again, she waits. On the third night, she is again abducted by "bearded, black-clad, wild-eyed warriors of Islam" (p. 273) and interrogated. Returned to Raqqa, she falls passively into the hands of Safia Bourihane, the now notorious agent of the attack on the Weinberg Center; and the two are taken to "Camp Saladin," just outside the ancient city of Palmyra. Here, yet another stage of Natalie's training begins, "her terrorist education" at the hands of Iraquis, "battle-hardened veterans" "who had fought the Americans largely to a draw in Iraq and wanted nothing more than to fight them again" (p. 288). Now Natalie has to don a heavy suicide vest and learn "how to arm the device and detonate it" (p. 289), a dreadful premonition of what will actually (nearly) happen to her. Yet once more, she is abducted and blindfolded, driven to Saladin's actual war camp, and taken into his presence, to discover that he is severely wounded and likely to die. This part of the novel is simply difficult to follow because of all the abductions and all the waiting, but it perks up when Natalie goes to work on Saladin's injuries and restores him to only slightly disabled health. Readers (and television watchers) love the special kind of suspense created by successful doctoring against great odds. And this blessing is reinforced by the allusion to Maimonides, famous medieval scholar and physician, despite the fact that, in truth, Maimonides did not minister to the real Saladin but only to his vizier.

I have summarized all this because it is tedious even in summary, and because in this novel, the idea of *waiting* has been raised to such a degree of intensity that it can no longer be seen simply as a device to create suspense. It becomes simply infuriating. Not only does Natalie, once back in the banlieue, have to wait for nearly three months to hear more from Saladin's camp, but we also never hear the message that directs her back to America—in business class! It appears that she has accepted Gabriel's plan to use her as a conduit of information about where the big attack will take place, but we do not hear his instructions to her; when she is waylaid by Safia Bourihane in a Washington hotel, it also appears that she has agreed to behave like a suicide bomber for access to information about what Safia's target is. Now Natalie seems to be in a trance, docilely doing or not doing whatever Safia commands, including not going to the bathroom! It is Haram, forbidden. What makes it worse is that when the two women don their explosive vests, concealed under their new fashionable jackets, the men watching—Gabriel, Adrian Carter, and the French and American presidents—decide not to intervene but to "let them run." And this after Gabriel, watching the vests go on "and while the entire counterterrorism apparatus of the United States looked on in horror," had declared, in the heroic and chivalric terms we have come to expect from him, "Get my girl out of there."

Natalie's guardians are completely blindsided. Not only have they failed to realize that Saladin's group had multiple targets, most of which are successfully wrecked with major loss of life, but they also managed to lose track of Natalie, who is foolish enough to be taken in by another woman who poses as FBI and delivers her to Saladin. Saladin admits to her that his use of her was, in any case, only a feint, designed to distract the antiterrorist executives; and it worked. How many mistakes can they make, one begins to ask? How could we trust them with anything? If this is how our anti-Isis strategists perform, we are in parlous shape. And within the fiction, Saladin himself has completely vanished, presumably to allow the series to continue.

But also within the fiction, they counted the dead: "One hundred and sixteen at the NCTC and the Office of the Director of National Intelligence, 28 at the Lincoln Memorial, 312 at the Kennedy Center, 147 at Harbor Place, 62 along M Street and 49 at Café Milano" (p. 484). The figures lend verisimilitude to what would otherwise be an implausible collection of locations, some symbolic, some merely places where civilians could be trapped. The President, who at this time is certainly Barak Obama, "refused to grant Isis its wish" for a final apocalyptic battle and merely ordered strikes "against all known targets in Syria, Iraq and Libya." Given the failure of intelligence demonstrated here, "against all known targets" is about as self-defeating a program as Silva could articulate.

Presumably this novel is intended as a warning: to the American President, against underestimating the danger of Isis; to counterterrorism experts against being too clever or *waiting* too long to make their moves; and to security outfits of all kinds and all nations against using women to infiltrate terrorist groups, *especially* if those groups are Islamicist with their inborn contempt for women. But what is the advice, going forward?

Gabriel's last (?) restoration, with which *The Black Widow* opens, is brilliant sleight of hand. In the first instance, it is *both* truth and fiction. The Caravaggio *Nativity with St. Francis and St. Lawrence*, stolen by the Mafia from the Oratory of San Lorenzo in San Palermo in October 1969, has never, in fact, been recovered. In fiction, it apparently had since at the opening of *The Black Widow*, Gabriel is working on it. If you remember in *The Heist*, Gabriel had discovered it, concealed by a "Crucifixion in the manner of Guido Reni, competently executed but rather uninspired" (p. 492), in the small church of San Giovanni Evangelista in Brienno, Italy. With his usual aplomb where matters of fact and fiction are to be distinguished, Silva tells his readers in his Author's Notes to *The Heist* that "there is no Church of San Giovanni Evangelista in Brienno, Italy. Therefore, Caravaggio's glorious *Nativity*, stolen from Palermo's Oratorio "in 1969, could not have been discovered hanging above its altar" (p. 494). In that note, Silva actually mourns the nondiscovery of the *Nativity*. "With each passing year, the chances of finding the large canvas intact grow more remote. The impact of its loss cannot be overstated" (p. 494). Yet here we are at the beginning of *The Black Widow*, watching Gabriel restore the *Nativity*, which by some miracle undescribed has been returned to the Vatican.

This truly is restoration in two senses. In the meantime, a real restorer, Adam Lowe, of Factum Arte, has been able to digitally produce a replica of the *Nativity* based on one small four-by-five color photograph taken by Enzo Brai in 1968. Technically, since the painting no longer exists but has been conjured up by Adam Lowe, it is as if we were indulging in a strange version of the literary device of ekphrasis, whereby words create for the reader the image of a painting he may never see or that, indeed, never existed. This case straddles both possibilities, making the fact/fiction divide more interesting. Caravaggio had defied tradition by making his holy family very ordinary people arranged in the most realistic manner with Mary seated on the ground in the center of the composition, clearly exhausted from childbirth, with the infant laid out on the ground almost between her legs. Two men who were identified only by the title of the painting as saints stand humbly on either side. It is not even clear who is the blond male figure with ostentatiously naked legs who sits on Mary's left side. Can this be Joseph, by tradition an old man? There is nothing marvelous about this birth, except for the beautiful angel boy swooping down from above, bearing a banner that proclaims, "Gloria in excelsis dei." His outstretched arms connect the earth below with the heavens above and formally mark out the strong diagonal axis of the painting, typical of Caravaggio.

The only concession that Silva himself makes to the ekphrasis tradition is to render this angel half visible to his readers: "an ivory-skinned boy who floated in the upper reaches of the composition . . . his right hand, which was pointed heavenward, was undamaged" (p. 45). This is clearly a reference back to the boy angel inserted by Gabriel into the clouds above his children's cribs, behind whom was Veronese's boy angel gazing down from a cloud in his *Virgin and Child in Glory with Saints*, behind whom was Dani, his dead son.

About The Paintings

This chapter began as an index to the individual paintings referred to in Daniel Silva's Gabriel Allon series. As the series continued, I realized that the concept of art and its restoration constituted more than a veneer over Gabriel's career as an assassin. The paintings selected for mention or for actual restoration tell us something about Gabriel that his adventures do not, hence something about Silva himself.

The game that Silva has been playing with his readers throughout, about the relation between fact and fiction and real-world events and distortions or predictions of them, becomes in the subtext of art a more difficult and sometimes frustrating challenge. Some of the paintings he introduces are "real" in the sense that they actually exist in some gallery and can be viewed today. Sometimes he tells us this in the "Author's Notes," usually in the most disingenuous manner. Some existed but have been stolen, some have been recovered, but Silva is not above recording fictional recoveries. The most extreme case is Caravaggio's *Nativity*, which remains missing, probably destroyed; but Gabriel first finds it at the end of *The Heist* and then, at the beginning of *The Black Widow*, is seen restoring it.

And of course, the "real" paintings are only images of the real (*The Pond at Montgeron*), and some are actual forgeries as when Gabriel forges a Van Gogh *Sunflowers* to deceive a criminal buyer or a version of *The Pond at Montgeron* to comfort the English Girl, who has spent so many hours viewing the original in the Hermitage in St. Petersburg but will now have to live with a copy of an image of a pond.

There is also the anomaly that Gabriel, an Israeli in the service of the Israeli state, almost always restores Christian paintings, some for the

Vatican itself, an anomaly noted by Shamron. The religious paintings fall into two groups: calm, highly composed scenes with *The Virgin and Child* and scenes of grotesque violence. Roughly speaking, he begins with nativities and moves on to martyrdom. Gabriel, or Silva, clearly goes through a Caravaggio phase, which concludes with the fictionally recovered altarpiece in *The Heist*, although this too is a *Nativity*, blending both strains. In addition, there is a secular phase, such as Van Gogh's portrait of Marguerite Gachet (a very complex case) or Rembrandt's portrait of Hendrikje Stoeffels or Mary Cassat's painting of two children playing on a beach, of which there are *three* versions, two forged or reimaged by Gabriel. It is made rather clear that these are women's paintings.

Though I am reluctant to mention them, along with deliberately misleading statements, there seem to be actual mistakes in some of Silva's references to or descriptions of paintings. Unless it is I who am mistaken.

But the mentions of descriptions of paintings lead to Silva's remarkable use of a famous literary device, ekphrasis, the conjuring up in visible terms of imaginary images, usually paintings. Perhaps less necessary in an age when reproductions are readily available online, ekphrasis has such complex nobility and genealogy (in Virgil and Spenser) that it deserves to be paid special attention.

So the catalogue, novel by novel:

The Kill Artist: A. *The Martyrdom of St. Stephen*, Vienna's Cathedral altarpiece. On page 1, Gabriel is restoring "a tiny portion of the painting just below an arrow wound on the leg" of the saint. But St. Stephen was killed by stoning as the altarpiece clearly shows. Silva must have been thinking of St. Sebastian.

B. Gabriel is restoring for Julian Isherwood a "very dirty" painting, "artist unknown," which he has acquired for a song and for which he already has a buyer, having recognized it as a Vecellio, that is, an *Adoration of the Shepherds* by Francesco Vecellio, brother of Titian (pp. 72, 94–96). He also claims that it is a lost altarpiece from the Church of San Salvatore in Venice. In fact, a very dirty actual Titian *Adoration* (1533) now hangs in the Galleria Palatina in the Pitti Palace in Florence. It appears to have a large unrestored patch above the figures. Francesco did paint four panels for the Church of San Salvatore, but they are on unrelated religious subjects. So this is all fiction.

Jacopo Bassano, *Susanna and the Elders* (1571).
Musée des Beaux-arts de Nîmes, France.

The English Assassin: A. We learn that Gabriel's share from the sale of the Vecellio, which took him a year to restore, was one hundred thousand pounds! (p. 16). Dispatched on a new mission by Isherwood, he finds in the house of Augustus Rolfe, the Swiss banker who has just been murdered, a Raphael *Portrait of a Young Man* for whose restoration his services had been summoned. "A striking image: a beautiful young man in semi-profile, sensuously lit" (p. 26). In fact, this magnificent portrait, believed by some to be a self-portrait, has not been seen since it was stolen by the Germans from a Poland gallery, a silent contribution to the theme of this novel, art theft.

B. As a metaphor for the Rolfe problem that Gabriel is trying to solve, he summons up the image of a Tintoretto he had once restored, a version of *The Baptism of Christ* that the Venetian master had painted for a private chapel. "Vast portions of the original painting had been lost over the centuries. Gabriel "effectively had to repaint the entire work, incorporating the small patches of the original" (pp. 262–263). Tintoretto painted this subject at least four times but never for a private chapel. The most likely version, and the most beautiful, is that in the Church of San Silvestro, San Polo (1589), previously overlooked, presumably because deteriorated, but successfully restored in 2004 with funding from an anonymous donor in honor of Frederick Ilchman.

C. The stolen canvases recovered by Anna Rolfe from her father's vault include "A Monet landscape . . . the Degas, then the Bonnard, then the Cezanne and the Renoir" (p. 289). The Renoir, "a portrait of a young girl with a bouquet of flowers" (p. 291), might be a portrait now in a private collection of a young girl in a black bonnet with a bouquet of tulips. The bundling of these together may demonstrate that Silva, and hence Gabriel, is not at this stage very interested in French Impressionism.

The Confessor: Gabriel's most important restoration, Giovanni Bellini's *Virgin and Child with Saints* (1505) altarpiece from the Church of San Zaccaria, Venice. "Widely regarded by historians as the first great altarpiece of the sixteenth century" (p. 29). Gabriel "never tired of looking at it. He marveled at Bellini's skillful use of light and space, the powerful pulling effect that drew his eye inward and upward, the sculptural nobility of the Madonna and child and the saints surrounding them. It was a painting of utter silence" (p. 30). Silva's first ekphrasis, a real painting in its proper place.

Later, Silva will use another Madonna and Child painting as a metaphor for the feelings of Tiepolo, head of the San Zaccaria restoration project, on learning that Gabriel is not Mario Delveccio: "It was as if he had just been told that the Titian altarpiece in the Frari was a reproduction painted by a Russian." Only a metaphor, yet Silva refers to a real altarpiece, really painted by Titian, for the Church of Santa Maria Gloriosa del Frari in Venice" (p. 357). The curious can find the painting online and see that it is the visual opposite of Bellini's still picture, for in the Titian (*The Pesaro Madonna*), every figure seems to be in motion away from a straight axis. The Virgin is leaning and looking down to her right. Silva has hidden a little lecture on art history inside a figure of speech.

A Death in Vienna: Giovanni Bellini, altarpiece in Church of San Giovanni Crisostomo, Venice (1513). Silva's second and most impressive ekphrasis:

> *At the left side of the image stood Saint Christopher, the Christ Child straddling his shoulders. Opposite stood Saint Louis of Toulouse, a crosier in hand, a bishop's miter atop his head, his shoulders draped in a cape of red and gold brocade. Above it all, on a second parallel plane, Saint Jerome sat before an open Book of Psalms, framed by a vibrant blue streaked with grey-blue clouds. Each saint was separated from each other, alone before God, the isolation so complete it was almost painful to observe* (p. 12).

The restoration of this "real" painting, in its proper location, both opens and almost closes the novel.

Prince of Fire: Rubens, *Daniel in the Lions' Den* (1615). Acquired by the National Gallery of Art in 1965. But Silva has it acquired by Isherwood for a song as by Erasmus Quellinus, identified by Gabriel as a Rubens, and shipped to him for cleaning. "The image of Daniel surrounded by wild beasts intrigued Sharon" (p. 397).

The Messenger: Daniel in the Lion's Den reappears as an "enormous canvas depicting a man surrounded by large predatory cats" (p. 13). When restored, it is sold by Isherwood for ten million pounds (p. 229). Not hard to see its oblique relevance to Daniel Silva and Gabriel's dead son, Dani, but Silva might have given us a better description. Rubens described this canvas as "Daniel among many lions, taken from life. Original, entirely by my hand." The lions used by Rubens as his live models were in the royal menagerie at Brussels. In fact, the lions do not look very scary, so that the miracle of Daniel's survival is downplayed.

Vincent Van Gogh, *Marguerite Van Gogh at Her Dressing Table*. This painting does not exist. It can, however, be conjured up as a slight amendment to *Marguerite Gachet at the Piano*, which Van Gogh painted in 1890 and can be seen at the Kunst Museum, Basle. There is a romantic legend about this and two other Marguerite paintings that they reflect a tender relationship between the painter and the young daughter of Van Gogh's doctor, which came to an abrupt halt, one that may have precipitated Van Gogh's drawn-out suicide later this summer.

The fictional version was supposedly owned by Hannah Weinberg and loaned by her to Gabriel to serve as a lure to reel in Zizi al-Bakari. Returned to Weinberg (p. 480).

The Secret Servant: The only painting in this novel is another Rembrandt, "a lovely painting by Rembrandt, appropriately called 'St. Peter in Prison,'" (p. 455). It is indeed a lovely and moving painting, showing Peter as an old man kneeling in a narrow column of light with his legendary keys on the floor at his side. Painted in 1631, it was gifted by Judy and Michael Steinhardt to the Israel Museum in Jerusalem in 2006, the year before Gabriel supposedly removed it for restoration. So no impossibilities here.

Moscow Rules:

Nicholas Poussin, *The Martyrdom of St. Erasmus* (1628), Vatican Museum. "A vast ghastly painting depicting a man being disemboweled . . . rendered in the style of Caravaggio" (pp. 20–21). Another commission from the Vatican succinctly described. Gabriel has worked on this before, and it is now shipped to him in Umbria for completion. It will again be deserted when Gabriel is summoned back to deal with the crisis of Ivan Kharkov and the "arrows of Allah." No doubt he was happy to abandon this disgusting painting, which shows the saint's long bowel being pulled out and wound round a capstan.

Mary Cassat, *Children Playing on the Beach* (1884), National Gallery of Art, Washington, D.C. This adorable if sentimental painting appears in the novel as its fictional twin, *Two Children Playing on the beach*, supposedly owned by Sir John Boothby and copied by Gabriel to sell to Elena Karkhov as a lure. Gabriel's version seems identical to the "real" thing even to the false craquelure he achieves by baking the newly painted canvas. Eventually, he paints yet a third version to comfort Elena, now safely in hiding in the United States, out of Karkov's reach. The children in the Cassat correspond to Elena's fictional twins who portend Gabriel's twins-to-be.

The Defector:

The novel opens with Gabriel in Umbria, restoring the Reni panel, *Crucifixion of St. Peter* (1604), also for the Vatican. It will be still unfinished in *The Fallen Angel*. But its presence here seems an excuse to reintroduce Caravaggio, who had painted the same subject three years earlier for the Church of Santa Maria del Populo. The challenge here was that St. Peter had asked to be crucified upside down so as not to imitate his savior. This allows Silva the chance for a double ekphrasis:

> *Before beginning work on Reni's panel the restorer had gone to Rome to view the Caravaggio again. Reni had obviously borrowed from his competitor—most strikingly, his technique of using chiaroscuro to infuse his figures with life and lift them dramatically from the background—but there were many differences between the paintings, too. Where Caravaggio had placed the inverted cross diagonally through the scene, Reni positioned it vertically and in the center. Where Caravaggio had shown the agonized face of Peter, Reni deftly concealed it. What struck the restorer the most was Reni's depiction of Peter's hands. In Caravaggio's altarpiece, they were already fastened to the cross. But in Reni's portrayal, the hands were free, with the right stretched towards the apex. Was Peter reaching toward the nail about to be driven into his feet? Or was he pleading with God to be delivered from so terrible a death?* (p. 16)

The question marks are crucial, bringing us face-to-face with the challenges of any attempt to interpret an image, especially one with a narrative (and a competition) behind it.

The Rembrandt Affair:

Rembrandt van Rijn, *Portrait of a Young Woman*, or a portrait of Henrikje Stoeffels, who is given a huge profile in this novel. Silva develops at length her fictional provenance, her use as the most expensive envelope in the world, its theft by a Nazi, her recovery and cleaning by Gabriel, and donation to the National Gallery in London by her owner, Lena Herzfeld. Silva's note claims that this painting "does not exist," but if it did, it would look markedly like the "Portrait of Hendrickje Stoeffels, which hangs in Room 32 of the National Gallery in London." This prestidigitation is self-mocking. A detail of the painting is tipped into the front of the novel with its identification and location. But the novel restores it to public view in 2010, whereas it was acquired by the National Gallery for ten thousand pounds in 1976 from the estate of Walter Morrison. Silva's first chapter is titled "Provenance," which makes fun of the very idea of reliability implied by the term.

Vincent van Gogh, *Self-Portrait with Bandaged Ear*. Stated by Silva to have been stolen by Maurice Durand and to be now "hanging in the palace of a Saudi Sheikh who had a penchant violence involving knives" (p. 79). Witty but untrue since one of the two versions of this self-portrait can be seen the Courtauld Gallery in London, and the other was sold at auction for seventy-one million to a Greek shipping magnate. In *The Fallen Angel*, Silva repeats this ridiculous story, now claiming that the painting was stolen from the Courtauld (see also *The Heist*, p. 158).

Claude Monet, *Customs Officer's Cabin at Pourville* (1882). In real life, owned by Steven Cooperman, who had bought it from the Montgomery Gallery in San Francisco and, in 1999, orchestrated its theft from his home to collect the insurance, a crime for which he went to prison. Its current location is unknown. Mentioned by Silva twice (pp. 48 and 491).

Portrait of a Spy:

Features a Titian, *Madonna and Child with Mary Magdalen*, acquired for Isherwood for a paltry twenty thousand pounds, sent by Isherwood to Gabriel for restoration, a process interrupted by terrorist activity in London. Sold at auction to Nadia al-Bakari at Christies "in order to channel several million pounds into the terror network" so as to destroy it. Returned to Isherwood, its owner, and donated by him to the National Gallery in London.

The Fallen Angel:

Caravaggio: *The Deposition of Christ.* Mentioned multiple times (pp. 12–14, p. 37, p. 289, p. 379, p. 393). Widely regarded as Caravaggio's finest painting," it is also clearly the most important painting in the Silva canon. Accordingly, it is given one of the best of Silva's ekphrases:

> *Nicodemus, muscular and barefoot, stared directly back as he carefully lowered the pale, lifeless body of Christ towards the slab of funerary stone . . . Next to Nicodemus was John the Evangelist, who, in his desperation to touch his beloved teacher one last time, had inadvertently opened the wound in the Savior's side. Watching silently over them were the Madonna and the Magdalene, their heads bowed, while Mary of Cleophas raised her arms towards the heavens in lamentation. It was a work of immense sorrow and tenderness, made more striking by Caravaggio's use of light* (p. 12).

The power of this ekphrasis is doubled by the affair of the *Euphronios Krater,* the great ancient artwork that initiates the theme of stolen antiquities; though this amazing object has actually been returned to Greece and is viewed by Gabriel in a Greek museum. "It depicted the lifeless body of Sarpedon, son of Zeus, being carried off for burial by the personifications of Sleep and Death. The image was strikingly similar to the composition of 'The Deposition of Christ.'" Veronica Marchese, the curator, states that without Greek vases, "there would have been no Caravaggio." Caravaggio, however, could not possibly have seen the *Euphronios Krater,* which was looted from an Etruscan tomb in 1971 and sold to the Metropolitan Museum of Art for $1.2 million in 1972. In 2008, it was returned to Italy, to the Archeological Museum of Cerverteri, where it can be seen today.

Also mentioned as incomplete Allon restorations: Guido Reni, *Crucifixion of St. Peter* and Poussin's *Martyrdom of St. Erasmus* (p. 13) (see below).

Caravaggio, *Nativity with St. Francis and St. Lawrence* (p. 76). The archetypical stolen painting that will be discovered in *The Heist*. The Reni *Crucifixion* appears again in *The Defector* (see below). The Poussin is mentioned again in *Moscow Rules* as being shipped from the Vatican for Gabriel to continue its restoration, which is again interrupted.

Paul Cezanne, *Mont. St. Victoire* (1895). Cezanne painted this, his favorite view, about sixty times. One version was stolen for Gabriel to blur the theft of a fifth-century terracotta Hydra by the Amykos painter (p. 170). Shockingly, he broke it into pieces as bait for David Girard, the crooked dealer in antiquities who funneled money to Hezbollah.

The Heist:

Paolo Veronese: *The Virgin and Child Appear to Sts. Sebastian, John the Baptist, Peter, Francis and Elizabeth* (p.16), ca. 1562, chancel of San Sebastiano, Venice.

The novel, which will be dedicated to art theft, begins with this painting safely in place and in process of restoration by Gabriel (p. 17). Silva provides only a brief and unemotional ekphrasis (p. 16) without commenting on Veronese's mastery of and specialization in the two-level painting, earth and heaven, connected here by saints looking up and boy angels looking down. This was a device important to Gabriel since he imitates it in his children's nursery. The main feature of the painting is St. Sebastian himself, tied to one of the central pillars that seem to support the Virgin and Child and indifferent to the few arrows that pierce his body, very much a Counter-Reformation painting and probably a response to the Council of Trent's third session (1562–1563), which endorsed the veneration of saints and martyrs.

But the setup for this novel occurred in *The Rembrandt Affair*, where Silva first introduced General Ferrari of the Art Squad, who has a replica of the missing Caravaggio *Nativity* behind his desk. The fictional recovery of that painting will be the grand closure.

In the interim, the novel introduces three paintings "stolen" by Jack Bradshaw or a henchman, hidden under copies of later works but revealed by Gabriel with his special cleaning method. Silva tells us all three were listed by General Ferraro as happily recovered. Here are the facts:

[Parmigianino] *The Holy Family* (1503–1540) stolen from Santo Spirito in Sassia, a religious complex near the Vatican, in 2004, reported by Ferraro as just recovered in 2014 (the time of *The Heist's* publication) but actually recovered in 2009 (CBC Arts), which also declared it not a Parmigianino but by the Flemish master Hendrick van den Broek. Silva must have missed that bulletin.

Pierre-Auguste Renoir, *Young Women in the Country* (1916), stolen in March 1981 from the Musée de Bagnois-sur-Cese, Gard. and not yet recovered.

Gustav Klimt, *Portrait of a Woman* (1916), stolen in February 1997 from the Galleria Ricci, Oddi, Piacenza, Italy (pp. 63–64). Not yet recovered though the search was reopened in 2004 in the hopes of identifying a partial fingerprint on the frame.

In his long list of notable recoveries, General Ferraro included Monet's *Beach in Pourville* (1882) stolen from a Polish museum in 2000, which was recovered ten years later but four years before Ferraro's announcement! And Modigliani's gorgeous *Woman with a Fan* (1919) stolen in 2011 from the Museum of Modern Art in Paris has not been recovered and was probably destroyed by the thief who lost his nerve.

If this does not serve to confuse you as to the relationship between fact and fiction in Silva's art history, then consider his use of Van Gogh's *Sunflowers*, "arguably his most famous work" (p. 154). Stolen from the Riksjmuseum Vincent van Gogh in Amsterdam by Maurice Durand's agent, it was used by Gabriel to create a forged copy indistinguishable from the original, whichever version could be called that. In fact, there were many versions of *Sunflowers*, one of which was indeed stolen from that museum on April 14, 1991, along with nineteen other works, all of which "were recovered from an abandoned parked car thirty-five minutes after they were stolen" as reported in *Crime Museum* at the time.

After *The Heist* and its amazing display of art historical (and not-so-historical) information, Silva seems to have tired somewhat of the motif. *The English Girl* is very short on paintings; though at the start, Gabriel is in the process of restoring a *Susanna and the Elders*, studio of Jacopo Bassano, property of Julian Isherwood. Unusually, Gabriel's reaction is focused on the story:

> *She seemed only vaguely aware of the two lecherous village*
> *elders watching her bath from beyond her garden. Gabriel,*

who was unusually protective of women, wished he could intervene and spare her the trauma of what was to come—the false accusation, the trial, the death sentence (p. 23).

Later, he imagines the English Girl whose disappearance he is investigating as Susanna with himself as restorer (p. 155). In the "Note," Silva plays his usual tricks. "The version of 'Susanna and the Elders' does not exist. If it did, it would look a great deal like the one that hangs in the Musée des Beaux-arts in Rheims" (p. 521).

Actually, if you consider the painting, you will see that Susanna is anything but "vaguely aware" of the elders. She is rather startled and afraid, gazing right at them. Bassano became famous for rendering biblical narrative in realistic human scenes with great expressive value.

Claude Monet, *The Pond at Montgeron* (1876), the Hermitage, St. Petersburg. Gabriel creates an exact replica of this painting to comfort his English Girl. This is one of four panels commissioned by the financier Ernest Hoschede, one of the first patrons of Impressionism, which is here represented in paradigmatic form, all lighted ripples. The barely visible sign of a woman in blue with a fishing rod, standing at the other edge of the pond from the spectator, could also be a statement about the insubstantiality of images. In the novel, however, it may stand for the loneliness of the English Girl and her importance to the plot.

The English Spy: There are no paintings here, real or fictional, except in metaphor. The cottage in Cornwall that Gabriel owns has loaned to Madeline for her safety is "perched atop the cliffs in the manner of Monet's 'Customs Officer's Cabin at Pourville'" (p. 33). There are fourteen versions of this view, which Monet painted in 1882, and a particularly beautiful one can be seen at the Metropolitan Museum in New York, bequest of Julia B. Engel, 1984.

The Black Widow: There are only two leftover paintings here and only briefly mentioned: Caravaggio, *Nativity with St. Francis and St. Lawrence*, fictionally recovered in *The Heist* and here given to Gabriel for restoration early in the novel (pp. 42–43); and Van Gogh, *Marguerite Gachet at Her Dressing Table* (p. 489), which was willed to Gabriel by Hannah Weinberg. When it arrives in Israel at the novel's end, it is gifted by Gabriel to the Israel museum, a fitting conclusion both to *The Black Widow* and to this chapter.

Printed in the United States
By Bookmasters